TREY

The Gates – Book 8

M. Tasia

ALSO BY M. TASIA

The Boys of Brighton series

Gabe

Sam's Soldiers

Rick's Bear

Jesse

Coop

Travis

Grady

Vincent

Shadow

The Holidays

The Gates series

Saint

Finn

James

Joey

Bradley

Carlos

Sawyer

EVERYONE LOVES THE BOYS OF BRIGHTON

"I loved this book and I love this town. I hope there's going to be more."
—Melissa Lemons on *Gabe*

"An amazing read that was filled with lust, love, crazy hot sex, danger, action and so much more This is the first book I have read in this series but I will definitely be reading more in the future."

—Gay Book Reviews on *Sam's Soldiers*

"I was crazy impressed that the author made me teary over the ending of a relationship that I shouldn't have even been invested in. I didn't yet know these characters yet the author made me hurt for them. That takes some mad writing skills!"
—Love Bytes Reviews

"Jesse and Royce together have my heart. Jesse has it all by himself."
—The Book Junkie Reads on *Jesse*

"So much action, intrigue, drama and angst for the long awaited story of Grady and Ben. This was worth the wait. Sexy and sweet. I can't wait for the next."
—SamD on *Grady*

"I knew this one would be my favorite to date! There was something about Vincent that said awesome then came Tristan."
—Booky on *Vincent*

"This installment of the Boys of Brighton was so good! I loved Shadow and Randy 's story I was hooked from the first page to the last. This book was definitely worth the wait!"
—AG on *Shadow*

"I have loved this series from the very first story and this holiday novella is simply perfect. We get a glimpse of all our couples and what is happening in their lives while the holidays explode around them. I cannot wait for more!"
—bookobsessed on *The Holidays*

EVERYONE'S NEWEST LOVE – THE GATES

"Having read the entire Boys of Brighton series, I was eagerly awaiting Saint's story and it was so worth the wait. I enjoyed every word. I am always amazed by authors that bring characters to life so much that you can hardly wait for the next story. Cannot wait for

Finn and Miguel to have their turn. While I'm waiting I'll reread the Boys of Brighton series!"
—Debbie Kay on *Saint*

"Ms. Tasia has done it again! This is Saint's story, for readers of the Brighton Boys, you'll know he needs a break! After being forced to become a plastic surgeon by his father, he rebels by assisting people in 3rd world countries, which puts him in the position to be kidnapped and tortured. You really feel for him, that's for sure! Max is the perfect man for poor Saint's battered soul, not that he doesn't have his own issues! Overall, this was engaging, steady paced and chock full of all the feels!"
—Avid Reader on *Saint*

"Finn and Miguel stole my heart. This is a great Sunday afternoon read. Finn's character jumped off the page as his story developed through each chapter. I loved reading his truth and watching him and Miguel find their home in each other."
—K.A. Brown on *Finn*

"Another tale from the Gates of Heaven, another two brilliant MCs we get to know very well. I loved both the plot and the characters, all their emotions and insecurities on full display. All the descriptions and world building were very vivid, providing a great background for an emotional story of self discovery and developing attraction."
—AL on *Finn*

"James...what can I say. I couldn't put it down. This is my first book in the series, so it definitely can be read and enjoyed as a standalone, but it will not be my last. Now I'm going to read the previous stories. Solid writing with a gripping style, characters that are right up my alley, and the kind of chemistry I love in my romances. What more do you need for a great reading experience."
—cinnamon on *James*

"This is really a great series and I def recommend it. I loved James and Ross, it was a rough start for the two, but they worked it out. I can't wait for more, love everything M. TASIA writes!"
—TammyKay on *James*

"I may have my new favorite book couple of the series. Joey and Sam just have that something special. At one point I was ugly crying but it was a good ugly cry if that makes any sense. I really love the series and I can't wait for her next installment!!"
—Vine Voice on *Joey*

"M. Tasia is an automatic 1 click author for me...she definitely didn't disappoint with Joey."
—Heather Weissman on *Joey*

"This author is really talented and I love her series, this one and the Boys of Brighton. Her characters are so well drawn and I can really get into the stories. I especially loved Eric in this particular book. I'm hoping Clay the rookie will be the next book. Keep 'em coming!"
—Rosemary on *Bradley*

"All the stories in this series have their own brand of excitement, this being no exception. All previous books include former heroes from the series which I find very charming. Our heroes here, Eric and Brad, give us another great performance. A villain surfaces and wreaks havoc on the lives of good people and is, after a stretch, put in his place. The book is a love story with a dose of excitement and, unfortunately, a bit of homophobia thrown in. A story nicely told."
—Tappy on *Bradley*

"Accompanying the gentle blooming of love between the damaged men, is gorgeous description. M. Tasia captivated me with her vivid illustrations of scenery and tourist sites (I feel as if I've explored CA and AZ beside the leading men), mouthwatering food, and intriguing art. I found myself wondering, is M. Tasia so well-traveled? A foodie? An art connoisseur? Or did she simply do her author's research very well?

Carlos is a tender romance coupled with mystery and suspense, not to mention several surprises at the end. In M. Tasia's words, "rebirth and determination" are a profound theme of the story, relating to people and places. This is a moving read, and a quickly devoured one, too, as it's difficult to put down."

—Kristen A. Remick on *Carlos*

"Carlos is ready to come out of seclusion. He wants to live near his brother, Miguel, experience the world outside his doors, allow the world to enhance his art. It's this brother who brings Clay into his life, a cop who quickly becomes Carlos' everything.

Two men with damaged souls come together and find love. A tried and true formula that works well here, especially when working with two lovable characters like Carlos and Clay. Carlos especially was interesting to me - the contrast of his appearance to his gentle nature, a true gentle giant. And Clay being all protective of the much larger, but more gentle man - so sweet! I really liked this story and am looking forward to more of The Gates now."
—Valeen on *Carlos*

"I loved this book and wish I had found this series right away from the first. I am eager to go back and read those works. This book was fantastic and I found myself enjoying it. There was a lot going on, but the author did a beautiful job flowing everything together. The characters were great and illustrated a lot of growth over the course of the story. I loved everything about this and found it difficult to put down. I look forward to reading more by this author. I give this a five out of five stars."
—Eliza Marie on *Sawyer*

"Sawyer is the newest addition to The Gates series. The book is very emotional, sweet, funny, romantic, and these two are great together. I look forward to every book in this series."
—Elaine Gray on *Sawyer*

www.BOROUGHSPUBLISHINGGROUP.com

PUBLISHER'S NOTE: This is a work of fiction. Names, characters, places and incidents either are the product of the author's imagination or are used fictitiously. Any resemblance to actual events, locales, business establishments or persons, living or dead, is coincidental. Boroughs Publishing Group does not have any control over and does not assume responsibility for author or third-party websites, blogs or critiques or their content.

TREY
Copyright © 2021 M. Tasia

ISBN: 978-1-953810-43-4

This has been possible because of the love and support of my family. Love you Craig, Samantha, Katie, and Jason.

ACKNOWLEDGMENTS

Thank you to my amazing publisher for taking the time to play tour guide in her diverse and stunning area of Southern California. Your indomitable spirit and strength inspires me to continue to grow as an author. Also, to my sisters-in-law, thank you for coming along and supporting my dream. The love and strength of family is the cornerstone of my career.

TREY

Chapter One

Perfect. Trey was in one hell of a mood.

First, he woke up in the hospital, surrounded by machines. Second, his left arm was handcuffed to the bed's metal railing. And third, he had some Scandinavian watchdog hovering around asking him questions about his part in it all, which he'd already repeated many times over. Were they trying to slip him up? Hell, he was telling them the truth.

This, right here, was what he got for having a damn conscience.

When he'd taken the job to find the location of Sawyer Hudson, Trey had honestly thought Cooper Hitchford wanted the address to serve the guy with legal papers. It wouldn't have surprised him if Cooper intended to sue Sawyer over the punch he'd landed, which the rich asshole more than likely deserved.

It wasn't as if Trey liked Cooper. The man was spoiled rotten to the core, but in a million years, he never would've guessed the guy would go psycho and try to kill Sawyer. After he'd confirmed Sawyer's location, Trey's take on the sitch changed when he met the whackjob Cooper had sent to replace him.

He didn't know his replacement's name or who he was, but one look told him everything he needed to know. There was nothing behind the guy's eyes. Dead and flat, they matched his stone-cold killer face. Which left Trey with no choice but to follow the creepy asshole around.

As it turned out, he'd been right to worry. Trey hated it when his gut proved right.

A sharp pain shot out from his telltale gut making him groan, and caught his babysitter's attention. On any regular day when he was out in the world, he'd welcome the attention of a handsome man. Not today.

"Are you in pain?" Detective Anders Nilsen asked. "I can get the nurse for you."

"Yeah," he grunted. Why lie? Hell, his pain was radiating so far across his body his hair ached.

"I'll be right back," the big oaf said. Apparently, they grew 'em big in Scandinavia. Trey remembered something about the people being descendants of Vikings or some shit like that. It was probably a stereotype.

He pulled on the cuff securing him in place as he thought about the people relying on him. Were they okay and worrying where he was? He tried to visit at least once or twice a week, and if he were destined for the penitentiary, he'd have to risk asking someone to look after them.

The door to his room opened, and the same nurse he'd met earlier in the day came in. She'd been the one who was here when he'd woke up for the first time. She smiled, but Trey was sure she had to be a bit freaked out about treating someone in handcuffs.

"Hello again, Mr. Stoneham. Let's get your vitals first, and then I'll give you the medication Dr. Green prescribed to help with your pain. It should help fairly quickly. The doctor is on his way to speak with you about your injuries."

"Thank you," Trey said. Why be mean? He might be having a shitty day, but she'd done nothing to cause it.

She went about checking him over, from his blood pressure to his bandages. There were so many bandages. A fire burned from where he'd been shot while trying to hold off Sawyer's kidnappers. In the end, Sawyer stabbed the hired gun, and Trey was the one to shoot and kill Cooper, which brought a host of new PTSD concerns to his already fucked up life.

He worried the cops didn't believe him. Like he was out for revenge after Cooper sacked him. They had to have Sawyer's statement, which corroborated Trey's recitation of the events. He didn't understand why they were up his ass. He tried to stay as close to the letter of the law as he could. His gun license and carry permit were up to date. His private investigator's license was current, and his record was spotless. Hell, he didn't take under the table money.

Like an idiot, he reported every cent he earned. Fuck of a lot of good it did him.

From the corner of the room, the Viking's ice-blue gaze was pinned on him, making him feel like a bug under a microscope. After Anders's introduction, they hadn't spoken unless the detective asked more questions, which Trey had stopped answering ten questions ago.

Why the hell was NYPD wasting a detective? The guy was sitting in a hospital room with a man who couldn't move without screaming out in pain. Like, duh. Walking might be a problem. He didn't see himself trying to make a break for it anytime soon.

"Okay, Mr. Stoneham, I'm going to inject the pain killer through your IV line," she said as she took the cover off of the needle. At least she was going to put it through an existing hole in his body without making a new one. He had enough of those.

"Please call me Trey," he offered in hopes of showing her he wasn't some hardened criminal or anything.

The nurse nodded her head and smiled. "You should be getting some relief shortly. I'll be back when the doctor arrives."

"Thank you." He wasn't going to be an asshole to the woman holding his pain meds. "I appreciate it."

She nodded, and walked back out of the room, leaving him alone with the Viking detective from New York City of all places. What was he doing here on the other side of the country over a relatively run-of-the-mill *I shot the bad guy before he could shoot me scenario?*

Figuring there was more to this story didn't bode well for him on a few fronts. He had an obsessive compulsion to research and dig things up. He loved chasing down a story, but digging into this detective spelled disaster, and he was no fool. Trey would give the guy a wide berth.

But it begged the question, what was really going on, and if it weren't the Viking sitting there, someone from NYPD would. Trey hated not knowing the whole story.

Twenty minutes later, Trey blurted out, "Why are you here? I won't be going anywhere for a long time."

"I'm trying to get a read on you," Anders replied, his voice cold as those fuckin' fjords.

"A read on me? What's so important about me?" There was nothing to "read" about him. He was as open book as you got.

Before Anders could answer, three men walked into the room, Dr. Green, he assumed by the white jacket, Detective Ross, whom he met before they threw him into an ambulance, and the big man who'd been doing security at The Gates, Miguel.

"Great, it's a party," Trey grumbled as the others stood back and the doctor approached his bedside.

"Hello, Mr. Stoneham. I'm Dr. Green," he said. "It's good that you've regained consciousness."

"Yeah, great," Trey muttered as he stared at the new arrivals. "See you brought along a couple of friends."

Dr. Green turned around and grinned. "Met them in the hallway. You seem to be popular today."

"If you knew 'em, you'd know it's not a good thing," Trey stated.

"I can ask them to leave if you wish to speak alone."

"Like Detective NYPD would leave me alone with you," Trey said and watched Anders for a reaction. Nothing. The man was made of ice.

"Has the injection eased your pain?" The doc asked while doing something on his tablet.

Trey took stock of his body and realized he didn't want to curl up into a ball anymore. A little good news. "Yeah. Actually, it has."

He nodded. "We need to talk about your injuries," the doc said as he scrolled down his tablet's screen. "The bullet entered your body under your right ribcage and went into your liver. We performed surgery to remove the bullet and stop the blood loss, which was flooding your abdomen. The bullet damaged a good portion of your liver, and we had to remove approximately thirty-five percent of the organ. You had to have two blood transfusions during the surgery. While it sounds dire, it went much better than we expected given your condition when you came in. We'll have to watch you to make sure that you don't get an infection or start bleeding again."

He knew a gut shot was a sure-fire way to get yourself killed, so he couldn't complain. Much. "Can I live without part of my liver?"

"In time, you should be able to go back to your normal life, and most of your liver will regenerate," Dr. Green explained.

"It grows back?" That was news to him, an organ that grows back. Too bad that didn't work on the heart.

"Yes, thankfully. We'll monitor you closely to make sure nothing goes wrong," the doc tried to assure him as he set down his tablet on the side of his bed.

"I'm not sure my life will ever be normal again," Trey said while clanking his handcuffs against the metal rail. "Things aren't looking promising."

"That's what's brought us here," Detective Ross said as he came over, slid a key into the lock of the handcuffs, and freed him. "You're not being charged, Mr. Stoneham."

Trey reached over—ow, that hurt like a mother— and rubbed the red mark where the metal cuffs had been. "You guys have such a sense of humor. You're free to go, but hey, you can't move anyway."

"I'll leave you to discuss this in private," Dr. Green said before turning and leaving the room along with the nurse Trey hadn't realized was standing near the head of his bed. He was getting really tired. Like, time to say *lights out.*

"No trick," Miguel said, though he didn't look happy.

Detective Ross gave the cop answer. "The DA said there's no case. No crime. Self-defense. You rescued Sawyer, directed police to the location where he was being held, and took a bullet trying to protect him. All upside for you."

"What I don't get," Miguel asked, "is why you cared?"

"What I don't get is why you don't get it?" Trey wanted to slap the big guy. "I was hired to do a job. When Cooper contacted me, I was led to believe I was looking for Sawyer for a pending legal proceeding. I mean, who didn't know Sawyer punched Cooper. The room was full of witnesses at a high-profile charity event where there were all kinds of journalists and television cameras. It wasn't a complicated connect the dots to *sure Cooper's going to sue.* Turned out, I was duped. I never thought the spoiled asshole had that crazy shit in him. But I knew something was up when I was dumped, and the guy who took over the case was a straight-up killer. I followed him, and the rest is history."

"Still doesn't answer my question," Miguel said. The guy wasn't giving up, and his holy than thou routine was pissing Trey off.

"I may not be a saint, but I'm still fucking human, with a conscience. I didn't want to see anything happen to Sawyer. Sure, being sued is shitty, but that's a far cry from what they intended to do to him." Trey had overheard Cooper and his hired gun talking before they realized Sawyer was gone. He never wanted to hear shit like that again. The hairs on his arms stood up at the memory, which he was sure didn't go unnoticed by the trio.

"So, it was a job to you, nothing more?" Ander's asked, joining in the bash on Trey party.

"Yeah. In the beginning. There's this little thing called bills that I need to pay. If I hadn't taken the job, someone else would've, and I doubt we'd be here discussing any of this today. By the way, Sawyer would surely be dead cuz no one else would've bothered to follow the killer." He pointed at his midsection. "What? This isn't proof enough for you, assholes?" Trey was slurring his words, was having trouble keeping his eyes open. Between the pain, the drugs, and this third fuckin' degree, he'd had enough.

"Believe what you want," Trey said, fighting to stay awake. "I'm the reason Sawyer is still alive." He flapped his hand. "I'm free. There's no reason for a police presence in my room any longer." He wanted to heal in peace and get a hold of *the family*. "Get the fuck out."

He wasn't entirely sure what he heard as he began to drift off. Something about a case and a bus. He was too far gone to understand, and he didn't give a shit. As long as they left and never came back, he didn't give two flying fucks what they were talking about.

***

Anders stood guard over Trey even though he'd been told in no uncertain terms to leave. When he'd first heard about Stoneham, he expected, well, an asshole. Not the straightforward guy with a serious gut wound lying in the hospital bed who had more than one nurse smitten. He was kind and patient with them even though he had to be in serious pain. Book/cover/judgment. Anders had been off by a mile.

Three days ago, while on vacation in LA visiting Ross, Anders received a call from his captain in New York regarding a case with a connection in LA. Anders wasn't thrilled to have his vacation thrown out of whack, but he looked into the matter. Trey Stoneham was the connection. He was linked to the New York case. Talk about a small world when the guy's name came up in the middle of Sawyer's kidnapping.

Anders had come out to holiday with Ross and his family and planned to stay with him at his house, but *all* of Ross's family was there. Saint offered Anders one of the empty bedrooms in the hub, a sort of dorm-like setup where Saint and Max, the owners, and Marian, the kitchen manager, lived while the building's top floor was being completed, and where they'd move to in separate condos.

The brief Anders had gotten from his captain put Trey Stoneham back in the middle of a nasty five-year-old case. There'd been a string of homicides in the lower east side of Manhattan, which had caught the media's attention. When the perp was finally caught, everyone learned he'd been Trey's roommate. Gary Olsen was convicted and sentenced to four consecutive life terms for brutally murdering four young women.

Trey and Olsen had been attending St. Joseph's College in Brooklyn. Trey was studying journalism, and Olsen was on the accountant track. Without Trey figuring out his roommate was up to something, finding evidence of the killings in their room, going to the cops, and giving his testimony at a sensationalized trial, the murderer might have never been found.

Anders was here today because Gary Olsen wasn't where he was supposed to be. He wasn't behind bars. He'd been on a prisoner transport bus, being transferred between facilities along with eight other men when the bus blew a tire. The driver lost control of the vehicle sending the bus careening into a deep ditch until it came to rest on its roof.

Three men were killed: two prisoners and the correction officer driving the bus. Olsen was missing. Apparently, being the upstanding citizen he was, he left everyone bleeding and dying, punched out a window with his feet, and fled. By the time the cops and the EMTs had arrived on the scene, Olsen had a half-hour head start. No one had seen him, and he was a fugitive being tracked by a shit ton of LEOs. He'd been at large for three days.

Anders had read the LAPD file on Sawyer's kidnapping, and had a hard time believing the facts of the case, especially as they applied to Stoneham. After rescuing Sawyer, Trey had gone back to the waterpark to stop Cooper and his hired gun from catching up to the kid. Trey'd had his car ready for Sawyer to make his getaway, and put himself between Sawyer and certain death. No two ways about it. Stoneham was right. Another PI wouldn't've followed the hitman, and Sawyer would be dead. The former Marine, Miguel, and all his buds from The Gates agreed with Stoneham's assessment, though Miguel didn't exactly communicate that to Trey. Once a Marine... Yeah. Hardass down to his toes.

Looking at the short, stocky man hooked up to machines, and a catheter drain—ouch—Trey Stoneham didn't look like Anders imagined him, and was nothing like anyone he'd ever met.

"You still here?" Trey's scratchy voice was barely above a whisper. His dark eyes squeezed shut as he tried to move, and he grunted. Yeah, total ouch.

"You want me to get the nurse?"

"No. I'd like to remain in pain and pass out from the agony." Anders turned, but before he could take a step, Trey said, "While I'm still awake, I'd like to get my point across since you didn't take the last hint. Leave. Me. Alone." He enunciated each word as if Anders was an idiot. He couldn't help the small smile straining at his lips.

"I'm afraid I can't do that," Anders told him.

Trey rolled his eyes, and Anders had to swallow his chuckle. "Why?"

Anders moved next to the bed. "Because Gary Olsen escaped detention and is currently missing." Trey's eyes went wide, and a bell began sounding from one of the machines, and Anders heard running footfalls coming from down the hall. "Hey. Hey. Are you all right?"

"No," Trey rasped. "I'm a dead man."

Chapter Two

He had to figure out how to get himself out of this hospital before Olsen showed up to carry through with what he'd threatened years ago. To kill Trey slowly and painfully. Yet another example of how doing the right thing was coming back to bite him in the ass.

Today marked the fourth day in his hospital bed. This morning they switched up the antibiotic they were giving him and upped the dosage due to a stubborn post-op infection, which was not uncommon with gut shot cases. Along with the bad news, he felt crappier now than he had a few days ago. Trey understood that he'd been shot in a vulnerable area, and it would take some time to heal, but going backward wasn't part of that plan. He was worried.

An officer was posted outside his room whenever Anders was away, which wasn't a lot of the time. As Trey was thinking of a way to get past his babysitter—yes, he knew that was stupid in his current position—there was a knock on his door, which was odd since he had no blood family who would visit, and Anders never knocked. Trey could have his butt hanging out, and the dude refused to leave. The word privacy had no meaning to him.

"Come in," he yelled, instantly regretting it as pain burst out through his stomach, which he was now clutching. *What the hell?* His knees were pulled up as tight as possible, and he rolled to his side.

"Are you all right, Trey?" Sawyer's voice broke through the fog of pain in his head. "Alexander, go get the nurse."

Trey heard the door open and close, and then something sounding like a small machine motor. He opened his eyes to find Sawyer and his brother Bobby hovering beside his bed. More people who thought he was an asshole and came to tell him. Perfect. Exactly what he needed when it felt like his gut was going to burn a hole through his back.

Before he could confirm their reasons for visiting, a nurse came in, followed by Sawyer's boyfriend, Alexander. She took Trey's vitals and injected something into his IV. He didn't bother to ask what the shot was. He figured it was pain meds. It'd been about four hours since his last dose, and they were pretty diligent about keeping him doped up.

"I'm going to call Dr. Green to come to take a look at you. I've given you a bit more pain medication to tide you over until he gets here," the nurse explained in a calm voice, but she couldn't hide the panic in her eyes. Shit.

"Thank you," Trey groaned. How could his gut feel worse now than when he'd been shot? This can't be happening. Hadn't he paid enough?

Once the medication began to kick in, he began to relax, and took in his three visitors' expressions of shock. Wonderful. He probably looked as bad as he felt.

Might as well get this over with. "Go ahead. We don't have to wait for the doctor to begin your beat down."

"Beat down?" Sawyer's eyes narrowed.

"You know, tell me what a shitty person I am, and how it's my fault you'd been found. Etcetera, etcetera." He figured their anger would be directed at him since Cooper was dead and unable to answer for his crimes.

"We didn't come here to do that," Bobby said, his eyes wide. "Dude, you saved my brother's life. I owe you everything for that."

Sawyer nodded. "I wanted to come by and thank you for everything you did for me. Breaking me out of that room and leading me to a getaway car. Then going back into that place to slow Cooper down from trailing me. Without you, I'd be dead."

A loud growl came from the big guy in the back. Alexander rasped, "Can we stop using that word? I don't want to hear how close you came to not being here."

"It's okay," Sawyer said as he reached for Alexander's hand. "I'm not going anywhere."

Trey watched the touching moment with the skepticism of a guy who'd been around the block, and had seen the worst of human nature. *It'll never last. Nothing ever does.*

He wasn't used to being on the receiving end of many thank you's and was at a loss for what to say. "Um… You're welcome." Pretty basic, but to the point. He wasn't known for his eloquence.

At their coordinating smiles, Trey figured he'd said enough to appease them. Besides, his stomach was on fire, and the throbbing took his breath away. The pain killer was helping, but he felt something wasn't right. This can't be normal.

"If you hadn't followed your suspicions, no one would have found me in time," Sawyer wrung his hands. Trey was sure the memories were haunting the guy. He didn't want to tell him they would for a long time.

"You're a hero, dude," Bobby said. His face was open and bright as if he'd won the lottery.

"Right now, I don't feel like much of a hero," Trey mumbled while trying to keep his breathing steady. He couldn't keep this up much longer. "This might not be the best time for a visit."

The door flew open, and Anders, Dr. Green, and the nurse came in. Even with the crowded conditions, Trey's vision was tunneling on Anders, as if the guy could make the pain go away. He had to be delirious.

"I'm sorry, you'll have to leave for now," the nurse said to his visitors. "Today isn't a good day for visitors."

Is he going to be okay?" Sawyer asked, making Trey even more nervous about what was going on inside of him. He didn't hear the nurse's answer before his visitors were out the door.

Dr. Green looked at Trey's vitals and then began removing the bandages from his abdomen. He looked concerned, and so did Anders.

Shit, what now? "What's going on?" Trey asked, tired of the silent treatment. "Am I bleeding again?"

"We're going to send you for a few scans to have a look at how you're healing. It appears your infection is progressing even though you're on strong antibiotics. We'll increase your dose after we get a blood sample to confirm my suspicions."

"Doc, I'm feeling worse than ever," Trey was positive something was wrong. "Do whatcha need to do."

After that, everything seemed to shift into a higher gear. The lab sent someone up to drain him of five vials of blood, and while they waited for the results, he lay in the cold tube of a CT machine.

Weird, but comforting, Anders was by his side the entire time. They'd even given the detective one of those metal aprons to put over his junk during the x-ray because he'd refused to leave.

Logical thinking had flown out the window when Anders's expression changed from icy and unfeeling to concerned and sympathetic. It had to be bad if Trey was being bombed with emotion from the cop.

Once he was settled back into his room, he passed out. The day had gone by in a blur and taken the last of his strength with it. When he woke the next time, he found himself in a completely different room. This one had wall-to-wall machines, more than in his initial room, and a glass wall through which he could see all the nurses and doctors working around a central hub.

Shit, this can't be good.

Moving his body was impossible. The blankets tucked around him made him feel like he was strapped down, and didn't have the strength to lift them from their serious tuck. It didn't take a rocket scientist to figure out he was in the ICU. What bothered him the most wasn't remembering how or why he was there. It was the constant beeping of the machines surrounding him, which was quickly pulling him back to sleep. He didn't want to go under. He'd lost so much time already.

"It's good to see you awake," a deep familiar voice said from the far side of the room, pulling Trey back from the brink of noddie-land.

Trey carefully turned his head to find Detective Anders sitting in one of those fold-down sleeper chairs. His clothes were wrinkled, his pale blue eyes seemed greyer than usual, and his five o'clock shadow had grown into a couple of days' worth of a beard. Gone was the polished detective with his starched attitude.

"What happened?" His throat hurt when he spoke. The last thing he remembered was returning to his room after a couple of scans. "The tests come back with bad news?" A stupid question considering his surroundings, but his brain was still trying to reboot.

Anders laughed softly and stood, stretching out his back as he did. "That's an understatement of epic proportions, my friend."

"We're friends now?" It had to be bad. "Am I dying?"

"What? No," Anders said. "Why the hell would you think that?"

Trey glanced around the room full of machines and turned back to Anders. "Oh, I don't know, Detective. You tell me?"

"To think I missed this abuse," Anders grumbled, making Trey smile and causing his cracked lips to tear in a few places.

He ran his tongue out over his chapped lips. His mouth felt like it was full of cotton balls covered in sand. "Am I allowed to have a drink?'

"Yeah. Far as I know," Anders said before reaching for a white paper cup and holding it up to Trey's lips. "Not too much you might make yourself sick."

He took a couple of slow sips, desperate not to make himself cough, but needing the cool, wet liquid to quench his thirst. Dull pain radiated from his abdomen, but Trey figured they had to have him on some serious medications because he wasn't curled up in a ball. Anders took the cup away and set it back on the bedside table.

"So, what happened after the scans?" Trey asked, his voice scratchy but better now that he'd had some water.

Anders moved the chair closer to the bed and sat down. That's when Trey noticed the time on the wall, 2:24 am. How long had he been out of it?

" Dr. Green discovered a small leak from one of the incisions on your liver. It was draining blood into your abdomen. It compounded the serious infection you were fighting. It came on so quickly it shocked the doctors. So, they went back in and stopped the bleeding, and have you pumped full of antibiotics. You're officially on the mend. The doctor was in checking on you about an hour ago."

"How long have I been unconscious?" Trey had a sneaking suspicion they weren't in the same day.

"Two days," Anders told him.

"Shit, the family must be worried sick," Trey spoke aloud, realizing his mistake the moment the words left his mouth.

"Family? What family? It states in your file you don't have any family left," the detective questioned. Since when did he have a file? Who created this file?

"I don't," Trey said honestly. It was amazing how many times people didn't believe him when he spoke the truth.

"Then what family are you concerned about?" Anders's withering look didn't shock Trey in the least. What shocked him was how much he wanted the detective to believe him, as if it mattered to him personally.

"Look, it's not anyone related by blood. Okay?" Trey explained while considering how much to tell him?

"Okay." Anders tilted his jaw up, daring Trey to refuse to tell him the truth. "Tell me who they are."

"Damn, man. I just woke up. Give the sick guy a break." Trey wasn't above using his current situation as a shield.

"You know I won't stop asking. Do us both a favor, save us time, and spill." Anders sat back and crossed his arms.

Trey didn't know what it was about the guy. Maybe it was cuz Anders had slept in that chair for the last two days. Or maybe it was Trey, and his concern for the family's wellbeing, which had him on edge, but who or whatever was the tipping point, something gave inside of him.

"Fine," he growled. "First, you have to swear on your badge what I'm about to tell you won't go into the 'file' you say I have."

"I can't do that if it involves illegal activity."

"Come down off that high horse before you fall, Detective. Heading to the worst-case scenario every time I tell you something isn't helping either of us. There is nothing illegal going on there. You'll see."

"I'll see it?" Anders asked.

"Well, someone has to go over there and let them know what's happening," Trey said, but quickly reconsidered. "Never mind. They'd smell a cop coming from miles anyway." Anders scowled. "Okay. If you go, you should take Finn and Marian. They'd understand better than you ever could."

"Does it have something to do with this?" Anders asked while holding up a crumpled piece of paper. "Sawyer gave me this to return to you and to ask if you still needed his help."

"I'm sure you've already checked it out," Trey wasn't a fool. "So tell Sawyer, yes please."

"That's the first time you've said please to me," Anders looked like he'd won some prize.

"I hate to burst your bubble, Detective, but the please was for Sawyer," Trey said. "Did you check out the address already?"

"Yeah. It's a two-story house in the Manchester Square area off Normandie Avenue on West a Hundred Forty-Fifth Place," Anders said while looking almost disappointed at Trey's earlier comment about who got the "please."

"Thorough," Trey acknowledged. "I'm surprised you haven't already done a drive-by."

With the slightest tinge of red to his cheeks, Anders said, "I have."

"Now that I believe. It may not look like much from the street, but it houses some important people. Don't scare them." Trey could imagine Ander's walking up the sidewalk all big, bad cop and pounding on the door like it was a raid or some shit like that.

"How would I scare them?" The towering man had the nerve to ask.

"Try smiling. Your scowl won't fly." Anders scowled. Trey wanted to laugh, but he knew it'd hurt. "And yeah, throw that judgmental tone out the window before you get there. Not everyone lives in your orderly world. If they need anything, tell Rachel to use the emergency money I left on the bank card in my wallet. I presume you have access to my belongings. Take the bank card to her. She'll do the rest."

The more Trey thought about what else he had to say, the harder time he had trying to remember everything as his brain got fuzzy, and holding his lids up was becoming a chore. He hated being helpless. With the last bit of energy he could muster, Trey said, "Take Finn and Marian. Please, Anders." When the guy smiled, Trey grunted, "Don't gloat."

"I'll tell Rachel, whoever she is," Anders promised. "And I'll give her the card."

"She's the glue." Trey's eyes were little more than slits. He was so damn tired.

Anders's eyes scrunched together, and for the first time, Trey noticed a tiny scar running along the top of his right eyebrow.

"The glue?" Anders asked.

"To everything." Trey closed his eyes, praying the next time he opened them, Anders would've spoken to Rachel. The detective had to do this for him, or people were going to suffer.

Trey had a feeling he was forgetting to tell him something, but he couldn't pinpoint what it was before he faded off into sleep.

It couldn't've been that important.

Chapter Three

The neighborhood appeared neat and tidy to Anders as he passed over clean streets, and by newly trimmed yards and rock gardens. The area was old, but well maintained, making him wonder what Trey had meant by *his orderly world*.

Zoning changes over the years were evident from the variety of homes. Small bungalows with one-car garages to sprawling two-story homes with two-car garages attached to the houses. The location wasn't in the safest part of LA, but Manchester Square was one of the nicer parts of its surrounding communities.

Marian and Finn sat quietly in the rental car Anders had picked up at the beginning of his *I had three days* Californian holiday as they drove to the two-story stucco home where Trey's family, but not family, lived. He'd figure out what the guy was hiding when they got there.

Different scenarios had been doing laps in his imagination, everything from a brothel to a cult. Even though Trey had said there was nothing illegal going on, it didn't stop Anders from thinking he'd been handed a pile of bullshit. Occupational hazard. He doubted Trey would've sent him in the first place if there was criminal activity. No one was that stupid. Then he remembered a case he'd worked on where the burglar happened to drop his wallet in the home he'd robbed. So yeah, there were stupid criminals out there.

All this shit was confusing the hell out of him. Who was the real Trey Stoneham? The ruthless journalist out for himself. The man with ties to the serial killer, Gary Olsen. The guy who led Cooper Hitchford to Sawyer, and then saved Sawyer's life to get himself out of trouble when it came out that he was involved from the start?

Anders couldn't pin him down to any one of those personas. He'd expected selfish, dangerous, greedy, and self-serving. Self-effacing, straightforward, and private? Ah, no. It wasn't in his temperament to trust easily. In his line of work, he'd learned sometimes the people who seemed to be nice and caring turned out to be pus-filled boils on the ass of society.

"It looks like a nice neighborhood," Finn, one of the managers at The Gates, said from the backseat. "Not what I expected."

"Speaking of not expected, we're lucky Miguel didn't follow us," Marian joked. "How did you manage to get past your overprotective husband this time?"

"I'll have you know I'm my own man," Finn blustered and stuck out his chest. "Miguel was on the third floor installing drywall when we left."

"That sounds about right," Anders said. That Marine dude was super protective. "He's not going to be happy when we get back."

"Yeah, yeah, yeah. So what do you think Trey's ties to this area are?" Finn asked. "I was told he grew up in New York."

Marian said, "This area is mainly working-class families, with some gentrified houses thrown in. Multiple generations living in the same house carrying out their version of the American dream. I used to have patients who lived in this area before I found myself on the streets."

"How'd that happen?" Anders asked as they stopped at a four-way intersection to allow a woman and two children to cross the street. The woman took a good long look at them as she held her phone to her ear. Anders always laughed to himself when people thought he looked suspicious.

"It's a long story, but suffice to say child psychology and therapy were a stressful career choice," she said, and nothing more.

Anders could understand. He had nightmares from cases involving children. They were always the toughest to get past after his part in the investigation was over. The department shrink told him some people never got over it.

Anders pulled over in front of a modest two-story, white, stucco house. The front yard was nondescript with nothing to call attention to it. There was an older model grey minivan parked in the driveway with two car-seats in the back. A collection of dents and scratches marred the faded paint surface, and he could tell there was barely any tread left on those tires. The house looked well taken care of, and friendly with bright yellow curtains hung in the front bay window.

"Okay, time to find out what has Trey Stoneham worried," Anders announced before reaching for the door handle and stepping out of the car.

Immediately he felt people watching them even though everything appeared quiet. His years of police work had honed several useful skills, one of which was being hyperaware of his surroundings. There may be no one out and about, but the community knew they were there, and it was watching.

Anders looked over at Marian and Finn, who seemed to be scanning the area along with him. "Feel that?"

"Living on the streets makes you sensitive to slight changes," Finn answered as he slowly turned his head to look behind them.

"I have no doubt we're being watched. No sudden moves, eh, Detective," Marian spoke in a conversational tone, knowing full well they were being listened to.

He wondered about her using his title. Trey was convinced the "family" would freak if they suspected he was a cop. Given the hairs on the back of his neck, he knew everyone who could see them was wondering who they were and why they were there. Inviting unwanted scrutiny wasn't smart.

"Well, since everyone seems to know we've arrived, let's go introduce ourselves," Anders suggested as he rounded the front of the car to come to stand by Marian and Finn. "If something goes down, here are the car keys." He handed them to Marian. "You and Finn get the hell out of here."

Marian looked at Anders strangely. "And leave you behind?"

"If I can't get to the car, leave without me," Anders stated firmly. "I'll try to buy you some time." He had his Glock under his jacket and wouldn't think twice about using it if his two sidekicks were threatened.

"You are certainly a puzzle, Detective Anders Nilsen. Much like Trey." Marian said. "Don't you think if they wanted us gone, we wouldn't have been allowed out of that car?" She took hold of Finn's arm, and they walked up the sidewalk side by side as if they were going on a Sunday visit. He'd liked Marian from the start. She wasn't anyone to be trifled with.

Anders followed them while keeping a close eye on the surrounding houses' windows for movement. Oddly, there was none. The envelope containing a note from Trey and his bank card was burning a hole in his pocket, and he wondered for the fifty-eighth time what was this "family" all about.

When they reached the door, Anders moved and stood in front of Finn and Marian in case they weren't as welcome as Marian made it seem.

He raised his fist and brought it down on the steel security door three times, and then waited. Anders could hear movement inside. Someone was home, and they had to decide if they were going to open the door or play possum.

After several seconds, the sound of twisting locks gave him his answer. By his count, six deadbolts were unlocked, confirming what was inside must be valuable. A straight-up hidey-hole. Whatever was going on in the house, he knew from experience: it could all go sideways in a heartbeat.

When the door opened with the chain-locks still attached, Anders could only see a small portion of the woman's face through the crack.

"Can I help you?" Her voice was strong, but Anders could detect a hint of fear.

"Hello, my name is Anders, and these two folks are Marian and Finn. We were sent here by Mr. Trey Stoneham."

He could see her eye widen through the sliver of the door opening. *Recognition.* This was the right place.

"Why would someone send you here?" Not admitting to knowing Trey. Smart.

Marian shoved against Anders's back and slid under his arm. "Let me through, you big lug. You're scaring her." She was remarkably strong for her age. "Hello, I'm Marian, and I'm sorry to tell you this, but Trey has been shot and is in the hospital. He was worried about you and sent us to check on you. He said to ask for Rachel."

"I was getting to that," Anders grumbled, looking down at Marian.

"You were taking too long," Marian griped and waved him off. "By the time you got around to it, that door would have been closed in our faces."

"I'm Rachel. Is Trey okay?" The woman in the house asked.

"He's out of danger now and has been moved from the ICU," Finn joined the conversation. "He's worried more about his family, as he calls you."

"What has that heroic idiot gotten himself into this time?" Rachel asked as she unhooked the shortest chain and opened the door enough for Anders to see her posture relaxed slightly.

"Can we come in to discuss this?" he asked, knowing there had to be more to this than what appeared on the surface.

Rachel held the door and said, "Give me a second." She closed the door, and one by one, each lock was opened. When Rachel swung the door wide, she stood over the threshold and said, "If you plan to cause any shit here, officer, it would be ill-advised."

Interesting. Anders hadn't introduced himself as a detective, but she saw right through him, or, more likely, overheard Marian's announcement from the car. Either way, Rachel reminded him of Marian.

"I'm not here to start problems. Trey asked us to come."

Rachel sucked in a deep breath before standing aside. "That's the only reason you're still here."

Anders led the way in case any unforeseen dangers were lurking inside. What he found was more shocking than he had ever suspected. Worried and scared faces were staring back at him. Women and children of varying ages stood or sat in the kitchen/dining room area. What the hell was going on here?

"Let's go sit in the living room," Rachel offered and began leading the way. "Jocelyn, will you please prepare a pot of coffee for our guests?"

"Yes, Rachel," a young woman answered while rocking a baby in her arms as she stood beside a fridge covered in children's paintings. This was not the scene he'd expected to find. He was having a hard time linking this place together with Trey Stoneham.

A hinge squeaked as Rachel led them through the kitchen's swinging door and out into a larger area containing a sectional sofa, multi-colored beanbags, chairs, and brightly painted stools for people to sit on. A newer television hung on the wall, along with well-used gaming machines underneath it. Toys were scattered about: dollhouses, race cars, and Legos. Yet, the place was clean and well maintained as far as he could see.

"Please, have a seat," Rachel indicated for them to sit down on the sectional while she brought a chair over and sat it in front of them. "Now tell me what happened to our Trey."

"He was shot trying to save someone he'd been following," Anders stated plainly.

"Sawyer, right. He was worried about that going south," Rachel said. "I had a feeling his disappearance had something to do with that case."

"He talked to you about it?" Finn asked.

"Yes, we talk about a lot of things," Rachel answered.

"What is your relationship to Trey?" Anders asked, unwilling to carry on until they had a few facts. Rachel seemed familiar to him, and Anders was wracking his brain, trying to figure out where he'd seen her before.

"We are friends and founders of what you see here around you," Rachel said while opening her arms to indicate the house.

"Founders of what, exactly?" Marian asked.

"This is a safehouse for abused women and children trying to get away from the violence of their lives and former homes. We offer an alternative away from the crowded shelters, where they could become further victims of violence. They stay here free, and everyone chips in with the care and maintenance."

Before Anders could ask more questions, like were they licensed, loud banging came from their front door again. "You expecting company?"

"Yep, and they're late," Rachel said as four large gentlemen walked into the living room, causing Anders to rise. If this were meant as an attack, he'd meet it head-on. "Where have you four been? Some psycho ex-husband looking for his wife and kids would have torn through this place by now."

"We were busy downtown," the one with the neck tattoo growled. "Looking for you-know-who."

"Well, you can call off the search. Trey sent these fine people," Rachel explained, causing two of the four to stand down.

"How do we know for sure they are who they said they are? That one there stinks of a cop." Neck tattoo guy pointed an accusing finger at Anders.

"I'm Detective Anders Nilsen." He held out his hand to shake, and the guy looked at it as if his hand might explode at any second.

Then he remembered he had something to do, turned and pulled the envelope from his pocket. "Trey sent this for you. He's included his bank card and said you knew what to do with it."

Anders handed the creased envelope over to Rachel, who unsealed it and pulled out the note and a bank card. She sat and read the letter, smiling by the time she was done, which made Anders wonder what Trey had written. "Always thinking about other people. He's up in the hospital with a hole in his stomach, and Trey's worried about making sure the mortgage got paid, and to get groceries for the children. He also said for us not to mind the big blond dufus."

The men grunted and shuffled forward as Rachel showed them the letter, making Anders feel a whole hell of a lot better about the situation, even though he'd been called a dufus. Her security walked back out the back door, and disappeared.

Anders sat as his mind raced, trying to place Rachel's face. He was confident that he'd seen her before somewhere, but where?

One of the women from the kitchen came in with a tray holding filled coffee mugs, a creamer jug, and sugar packets. She placed the tray on the coffee table, and left the room, eyeing Anders as she returned to the kitchen.

When he heard the door swing shut, he asked Rachel, "What you're telling me is Trey gives you money to run a shelter for women and children, and you're its caretaker, and those," he pointed to the back door, "thugs are security?"

"That about sums it up," Rachel said, crossing her arms daring Anders to find anything wrong with that.

"I have one more question," he said. "Who are you?"

Her eyes lit up at the question. "I was wondering when you'd get around to that, *New York* Detective Nilsen. My legal name is Rachel Anne Olsen."

Anders felt a lead weight fall into his stomach. Rachel was serial killer Gary Olsen's mother, and he'd seen her in pictures from her son's police file. What were the odds that the mother of Olsen, and the roommate who helped put Olsen away were here on the west coast and working together?

Slim to none.

"That's going to require a bit more information," Anders stated. "Have you heard from your son?"

"Gary? Not since the day he was sent to prison." Rachel looked repulsed by the question.

"Are you aware that your son has escaped custody and is currently the subject of a nationwide manhunt?"

Rachel went white. Her expression changed in an instant from disgusted to frightened. "How the hell did he escape? How long has he been out there? Have there been any sightings?"

Marian stood and went to comfort Rachel. "It'll be okay. They'll find him."

"He'll come for Trey, and even me if he has the slightest chance," she whispered. "The women and children here could be hurt if that happens."

"I'll talk to the LAPD. One of the detectives is a good friend. I'm sure he could arrange for a patrol to do sweeps by the house," Anders offered. "My guess, if LAPD or the county sheriff's office gets word your son is in the area, you'll be notified ahead of time." He dug into his back pocket and pulled out his wallet. "Here's my card. It has my cellphone number written on the back. If anything out of the ordinary happens, call me, and I'll let Detective Ross know immediately."

Rachel took the card and examined it like a bug under a microscope. "Do you intend to kill him, Detective Nilsen?"

"No, I intend to take him back into custody, and return him to New York state to resume his prison sentence." Deadly force was a last resort, and Anders didn't want any violence, especially around this house.

"That's what I thought," she said in a much stronger voice. "You can't do what needs doing. Gary deserved the death penalty, but he got life without a chance for parole. Now, look where we are. He's a psychopath with a taste for blood. He won't stop until he's dead," she stated with conviction. It was odd to hear a mother talk that way, but considering what her son had done, he understood.

"Be safe. Make sure that security of yours keeps an eye out for anything unusual. Don't place yourself in danger to catch him, and don't go out in public where he'll have a shot at you. Send someone from your security crew to get the groceries and necessities at least until Gary is found."

"We'll be on alert," Rachel assured.

Anders had to know. "One last thing. How did you and Trey end up on the other side of the country together and running a women's shelter?"

"People deal with guilt in unexpected and unorthodox ways." Rachel's eyes looked weary for a moment before her determined gaze returned.

"But neither of you were found to have known anything about what Gary was doing? You both testified to put him away." Anders didn't understand why they'd have any feelings of guilt.

"True. However, knowing that monster lived among us day after day, and we were oblivious to his evil. Not knowing when we feel we should've, carries its own level of guilt."

"A penance," Finn announced.

She nodded. "It's our penance for not realizing and stopping Gary sooner. Now, we dedicate our lives to protecting as many women as we can. But it's never enough."

Anders wasn't sure what he was feeling. Confused, guilty for expecting the worst, angry, these measures were needed to protect those women from the men who said they loved them. Along with worry for the safety of those living here, if Gary Olsen ever found this location. Anders was double worried Trey would put himself in front of a bullet to keep the bastard from hurting anyone in this house.

Two little legs came waddling out of the kitchen and straight for Anders. The infant lost her balance when she was a few feet away, but he caught her before she had a chance to fall.

Her beautiful, dark brown eyes looked up at him with the innocence only a child could possess. Chubby arms spread out wide, and her hands went into the air, the classic "uppie" move. Anders lifted her and placed her on his knee. Her pink onesie declared the little girl a Princess, and he had to agree. All the cutie needed was a sparkling tiara.

At that moment, Anders understood why Rachel said what she did about ending the murderer's life if he got anywhere near this house. Funny, in a way, he'd been right from the start.

This house contained something precious indeed, and they needed protection.

Chapter Four

Trey woke to find somebody had turned all the lights off in his hospital room. His eyes were blurry, and his mind cloudy in the first few seconds of wakefulness. Since his second surgery, he was out of the ICU and on the mend, feeling healthier every day.

Anders hadn't come back since his visit to Rachel's house days ago, and Trey couldn't help but worry something had gone wrong. He'd forgotten to inform the detective of who Rachel was and the added security in place, but figured since Finn had called and told Trey everyone in the house was safe and Rachel had the card, he didn't need to lay awake worrying himself sick again.

Reaching for the bed rail, he pushed the button to raise the head so he could sit up, at least partially. It had been getting less painful to bend his abdomen as the days passed, a sure sign he was heading in the right direction. That was when he noticed a black cardboard box on his bedside table, about the size of a tissue box. Trey was sure it hadn't been there when he'd fallen asleep hours earlier.

He looked around his room. Same off-white walls, faded bed curtain, and windowless cave he'd come to expect. Everything was the same, making him wonder who'd visited him while he'd been sleeping. He reached over to examine the box. There were no markings to indicate where it might have come from or a note saying who'd left it. He was about to remove the lid when a nurse walked into his room, rolling the cart with the laptop computer on it. She squirted sanitizer on her hands, rubbed them vigorously, then pulled on blue nitrile gloves.

"Good to see you awake," she said. "On a scale of one to ten, how's your pain level?"

He shrugged. "I dunno. About a five or six, I guess."

As she typed on the keyboard, she asked, "How do you feel?"

"Much better with every day that passes." He pointed to the tilt of the bed and said, "I couldn't sit up this far yesterday." She nodded and kept typing. "It looks like I had a visitor," he told her while grabbing for the lid to the box.

She frowned, turned for a moment to scroll through the screen. "It doesn't say anything here about a visitor."

Trey had to wiggle the lid to remove it from the box, and when he finally could see what was inside, he was struck speechless. On top of a fast-food napkin stained red was a finger, and by its size, shape, and glittery pink nail polish, it had come from a woman. The nurse screamed and ran out of the room. He couldn't blame her. If he could run, he would've joined her.

As the police officer stationed at his door came running in, Trey noticed handwriting on the inside of the lid. It read, "See you soon. Love, Gary."

Fuck. He's found me.

***

Officers crowded the hallways as Trey was moved far from where he'd been and was placed in a room in the far corner of the ward where the two new officers he'd gained were standing guard outside his door. He had yet to see Anders, who probably was out looking for Gary.

Trey didn't want to examine too closely why it made him angry the guy hadn't called or checked in. The least he could've done was say goodbye, especially after making such a fuss about keeping an eye on him. Not to mention sharing the safehouse with him. Trey fought against emotions he'd buried long ago, and he'd be damned if one callous New York detective would stir up shit Trey had no intention of examining.

He'd trusted Anders with a piece of his life he shared with nobody. Not coming by after having gone there, felt like a betrayal.

Well, fuck Anders Nilsen. Trey had bigger fish to fry with Gary wandering around the hospital without anyone noticing. The doctor had checked on him, and he was doing better. Trey had to figure out how to get away from this hospital before Gary came back. Obviously, the psycho could get in here. How in the hell had he gotten so close to Trey with a cop stationed by his door since day one?

Maybe the cops were using him as bait. When Gary came to finish Trey off, the cops could arrest him. Nice. He was a sitting duck. Literally.

Moments later, the door to his room swung open, freaking Trey out even though he figured Gary was no longer in the building. No doubt, he was long gone before Trey had opened the box. This time around, the group contained the disappearing detective, along with his doctor, Detective Ross, and Miguel, of all people.

"I see you're still around, detective," Trey said as Anders neared his bed.

"I've been busy," he answered. "Did you miss me?"

"Fuck no." *That would be the day.*

"Couldn't stay out of trouble while I was away, I see," Anders shot back without even looking up from whatever he was reading on his phone.

"Hey, I didn't have anything to do with this, you Viking asshole." There was no way he could blame this on Trey.

"Viking asshole? That's all you got?" Anders looked amused.

"Would you prefer troll?"

"It would be in keeping with my Norwegian heritage."

"I'm a little hard up for comebacks at the moment; I can't seem to put a *finger* on why that is," Trey said while waving a single finger at them. The cops may be used to seeing blood and gore. Trey wasn't, and never wanted to be.

"Yeah. Let's discuss the finger and your visitor," Detective Ross said. "What did you see?"

"Nothing, I was asleep. Where the hell was my guard?" Trey asked.

"Indisposed," Anders said with a growl.

"He was in the restroom?" Trey coughed, and damn that hurt. "You've got to be shitting me, pun not intended."

"This is serious," Anders admonished as if he were a naughty child.

Trey saw red. "You don't think I'm taking a murderous psychopath leaving a woman's severed finger in a box beside my bed while I was sleeping, seriously?" How had his voice gotten so high? He was yelling. "Are you fuckin' with me right now?"

"Easy, Mr. Stoneham. Please calm down," Doctor Green said while looking at the monitors. "You're recovery could be jeopardized."

Trey's machines were beeping louder than they had a few moments ago. Of course, he was upset, but he had to get himself together. Trey needed his strength for whatever Gary had in mind. When it came down to it, Gary would make sure he looked Trey in the eyes before the end came.

Anders sucked in a deep breath and let it out slowly while Detective Ross and Miguel watched on.

"What?" Trey asked Ross and Miguel, seeming to snap them back to the here and now. "Do we even know which poor woman was attached to that finger?"

"We'll be running the fingerprint in hopes of identifying her," Detective Ross said. "In the meantime, we need to place you into protective custody."

"Isn't that what I was supposedly in already?" Hell, what did they call the cops standing outside his door? His Maître Ds?

"This will be in a secure location, not the hospital," Anders clarified. "There are too many variables here."

"Yeah, like my last gatekeeper's bowels." He waved a hand toward the machines and the lines to his body. "You're seriously thinking of removing me from the hospital? Isn't that counterproductive to my continued recovery?" Trey didn't want to go backward again. One brush with death was enough, thank you very much.

"You'll be under medical supervision the entire time," Detective Ross stated. "Miguel has been trained as a medic while serving in the Marines Corps. You'll be in good hands."

Trey glanced over at the big guy standing quietly in the corner. "You sure about that? He looks like he'd sooner eat nails."

There was a slight tick in the corner of Miguel's mouth, but that was it. Terrifying, dude.

"I'll be there as well to keep an eye on you," Anders said. "Lord knows the shit you could get into."

"Keep an eye on me? I'm the victim in all of this. Stop treating me like the criminal, Detective Nilsen." Of course, his machines began their ringing and buzzing chorus again.

"If you two can't be near each other without arguing, I'm going to have to recommend removing Anders from this aspect of the case." This time both he and Anders turned to look at Detective Ross. "I'm serious."

"Fine," Anders grumbled. "I'll be with Miguel to protect you."

"Fine," Trey growled back. "How hard was that?"

Anders's head fell back on his shoulders as the big guy stared at the ceiling and groaned.

"Okay, we'll begin arranging the transfer," Doctor Green said. "However, if at any time Trey's condition changes, he must be brought back into the hospital immediately."

"Agreed," Anders said. "We'll be in daily communication with you, doctor."

"Good," Dr. Green said before walking out the door.

Funny, no one asked Trey what he wanted to do, and by the action picking up around him, he doubted anyone would.

Instead of arguing, he laid his head against the pillow and closed his eyes, allowing the world to flow around him. The tumult and terror were proving too much for his weakened body. Within minutes he was nodding off, even though he'd woken less than four hours ago.

He hated being weak. Society ate up the weak, and he refused to be its victim.

***

"Are you sure about this, man?" Anders asked as the ambulance pulled up to the back of The Gates building. He and Ross had followed behind in an unmarked police cruiser. "We thought Trey was safe in the hospital, and Olsen still got in."

"This place has been outfitted with top-of-the-line, cutting edge security features. Saint had the building made impenetrable before they even threw the first hammer in restoration. The Sentinels set it all up for him," Ross explained. "While, of course, the lounge and restaurant areas are open to guests, the private areas are sealed off." Anders remembered Ross mentioning Saint had been kidnapped once while in another country and honestly understood his need for safety.

Anders and Ross had started their policing careers together in New York City and spent a few years in the same unit before Ross accepted a position in Los Angeles. They'd kept their friendship alive even though they were on opposite sides of the country. Ross was like a brother to Anders, and he'd hate to lose that, considering all of his family lived in Norway.

"The Sentinels?" Where had he heard that name before? "That's familiar."

"They're a group of retired military personnel who now work in private security along with several government contracts mixed in. Their group is based out of a town called Brighton in the Texas Hill Country. Miguel's done some work with them in the past."

Anders took another look at the limestone building he'd been calling home since his arrival in LA. With his vacation hijacked by Olsen's escape and everyone's worry over what the psycho might do to Trey, Anders was assigned to bodyguard duty while the LAPD and LA county sheriff's office were investigating people and places Olsen might go. Everyone was in agreement. Olsen would set his sights on getting even with Trey.

Anders thought it was too obvious for Olsen to come directly at Trey, but he didn't put it past the psycho to have someone do his dirty work for him. They weren't sure that wasn't what happened today. Olsen could've signed the box and handed it off to any number of people. LAPD was checking the security footage on the floor where Trey had been, but so far, they hadn't spotted Olsen, or anyone else who looked out of place. Widening the search in such a big institution was a lot of ground to cover.

He was totally pissed off the officer on duty had left his post. Anders couldn't help but wonder how long Gary, or whoever had done his dirty work, had been watching Trey's room for his chance. Since Trey was asleep, why hadn't Olsen or his lacky done what he'd sworn to do? Kill Trey.

Of course, he didn't want Trey to get hurt. Hell, he was beginning to almost like the guy. But Gary had something planned, and Anders had to figure out what that was before it happened.

"Look, buddy," Ross said as Anders parked the cruiser off to the side. "If you're truly pissed at having to watch over Trey, I could arrange for someone else to take over."

Anders turned to look at his friend as if he'd lost his mind. "I didn't say that." Where the hell did Ross get that idea?

"You didn't have to say anything. The way you two talk to each other, damn. There's no love lost between you guys." Ross shook his head.

"I'm not going anywhere," Anders stated. "Gary Olsen will have to go through me to get to Trey."

Ross's head snapped around, and he eyed Anders in confusion. "Let's hope that never happens, but what gives? One moment you can't stand being in the same room as Trey Stoneham, and now you'll take a bullet for him?"

Anders quickly looked away. "It's my job. Trey is our best shot at catching Olsen."

"Your job, right," Ross grumbled. "If you need someone to talk to about this shit, you know you got me, right?"

"Talk to? What, are we doing yoga next? This Californian life realign your chakras or some bullshit?" Anders couldn't help but smile as he jabbed his friend. "Yeah. I know that, man. Thanks. Let's go make sure Trey gets settled in, or I'm sure we'll hear about it."

They both reached for their door handles and exited the vehicle, and with a nod from Ross, the paramedics had Trey wheeled inside The Gates fast. They'd decided to put him in one of the spare bedrooms in the hub beside Anders temporary room. Trey remained quiet throughout the ordeal, and Anders worried all the jostling and stress since Trey discovered the finger would set back his recovery.

Miguel cataloged every machine being set up and triple-checked the wires and tubes leading from them to Trey. The Marine seemed to have a handle on keeping Trey healthy, so Anders excused himself to search out Saint.

He found the owner of The Gates in the hub living room area talking to Marian. Saint was carrying a few cardboard tubes under his arm and a coffee mug that said Best Boss in his scarred hand.

"Hey, Anders," Saint said as he neared them. "Everything going okay?"

"Yeah. Not a hitch," Anders said. "Thanks again for allowing Trey to bunk here."

"No problem. From what Marian and Finn told me about Trey, he's welcome at The Gates anytime."

"I was hoping to ask if I could look over the drawings of the buildings, including the security system. It's not that I doubt the security, but I need to be prepared for anything."

"Of course," Saint said as he lifted the cardboard tubes. "That's what these are. I thought you might want to have a peek at them."

"Thank you." Anders reached for the tubes and tucked them under his arm. "I'll get them back to you as quickly as possible."

"No rush," Saint said. "How's Trey doing?"

"Fine," Anders answered on autopilot while looking around for a large table on which to roll these drawings out.

Marian shook her head slowly. "It must be terrifying for Trey. Cooper almost killed him while he was saving Sawyer and then finding a madman's calling card less than a foot away from him in what was supposed to be a secure room. Every time that boy tries to do something good, it blows up in his face."

"Something good? The guy's not some saint." Then he looked over at Saint. "Sorry."

"Huh?" Marian looked at Anders like he'd grown two heads. "You forget he helped put a serial killer behind bars? Then he teams up with the killer's mother and sets up a shelter to protect battered women and children. He had to take any job that came his way to earn money to support and maintain the shelter, only to have the job turn south on him. He saves Sawyer and gets himself shot in the process, almost ending his life. Which now endangers his ability to continue supporting and saving these women and children," Marian drew her brows together. "Did I miss anything, Detective?"

Why was she so passionate about this? "He's also the same person who sent Sawyer into hiding with his article in the newspaper about a love triangle between Cooper, Alexander, and Sawyer. He spends his days lurking in the shadows, following people, and reporting on them. Forgive me for not hopping on the bandwagon quite yet. Trey Stoneham isn't as innocent in all of this as you might think."

"You might have to wait and see, but I'm convinced." Marian smiled wide. "Until then, maybe you should keep a close eye on him."

"I intend to. Don't worry." Nothing was going to get by him.

"Good," Marian said. Anders had to wonder why she was still smiling. Like she knew something he didn't. Anders didn't like it.

All this California touchy-feely shit. Trey was a case, nothing more. Anders didn't wear rose-colored glasses. They'd been ripped from his eyes long ago, and this pseudo hero wasn't about to change that fact. Anders would do his job and then get his ass back to New York. He missed everything about the city. There was nowhere like it in the world.

Chapter Five

Trey had been at The Gates for a handful of days, and was no closer to figuring out a way to leave this building. What had they been thinking when they brought him here? Now, there were more innocent people in the line of fire. He'd been stewing on the lack of tactical brilliance for days and was no closer to a solution.

Miguel turned out to be a great doc even if he barely spoke. Marian visited daily, and she made up for any lack of chatter. Sawyer and Finn stopped by a few times to check in, and both were friendly and out-going. Slowly he was getting to know The Gates' crew on a more personal level than he had when he'd been surveilling the building. It was hard to believe what a difference a month could make.

A large man named Carlos had come by with his fiancé Clay and left Trey a sketch pad and colored pencils to help keep him busy. Carlos was Miguel's brother and an artist. Trey had used his phone's browser to search out his work. Stunning stuff. No other word fit what he saw. How a single person could create such beauty while another only knows destruction? Trey would never understand what went on in people's brains.

Anders had set up a chair and a small desk with a lamp in the far corner of his room so the overhead lights could be turned off when Trey was asleep. The detective was always busy doing something, and spent most of his time ignoring Trey.

Rachel had called to reassure him everything was fine at the house, and they were keeping an eye out for Gary. One thing was for sure—Gary wouldn't be able to waltz into that neighborhood unannounced. At least Rachel, the houseful of women, and the children were safe.

Trey stared at the same two spots on the ceiling as he thought about the day his life changed forever. The day he discovered what his roommate had been hiding in his room. He couldn't stop the chill running through his body at the painful memory.

"You all right?" Anders asked from his corner. He far enough away to make Trey wonder how the detective had noticed such a small thing as a shiver.

"Yeah," he replied. "Thinking over things."

With one raised brow, Anders said. "Don't worry. We'll catch Gary before he has a chance to harm you." A monotone, rehearsed line if he'd ever heard one.

Did the guy ever come out of his cold professional detective mode? "For your information, I wasn't worried about Gary. It's inevitable he'll find me."

"What were you thinking about?" Anders asked, apparently ignoring the last part of Trey's sentence.

"The day I discovered I was living in the same apartment as a serial killer." That got the detective's attention, and it only took murder and mayhem to do it.

"How'd you find out?" Anders asked. "The case file says you called police while your roommate was away from home."

"Yeah. He was going out to dinner after classes that day." Trey could remember it as if it were yesterday. The setting sun, dripping kitchen faucet, and jazz music was coming from the apartment upstairs.

"At that private school you two attended in Brooklyn." Trey didn't miss the snideness in Anders's voice.

"Yeah, that hoity-toity private school where my great aunt worked in administration for over thirty years, which allowed me the opportunity at a higher education I couldn't afford otherwise."

There was a slight change in Anders's expression, but it was gone as quickly as it arrived. "So what tipped you off about Gary?"

"He'd always been odd and not in a quirky loveable kind of way. I needed a cheap room to rent near the school, and he had one." Amazing what you'd put up with when you had no other choice.

"So you took it even though you had misgivings? Seems unwise."

"Yeah, it was. But some of us don't have the option to be picky. I was fortunate enough to attend there. The grant didn't include room and board. I was the school's charity case they could bring out and parade around when media came by to show their civic awareness."

"Didn't that bug you?"

"Yeah, it did. The administration would dress me up in hand-me-down suits and parade the charity case before donors, like the underprivileged kid I was. Really, who gave a shit? I kept my eyes on the prize. My degree in journalism from a highly ranked east coast private school." That alone should have written his ticket to any newspaper. He'd been so näive.

"Why journalism?"

"I've always been curious. I used to drive my mom crazy when I got the neighborhood scoop before she did. It seemed a natural progression. Unfortunately, any hard-hitting, entry-level journalism positions I applied for shied away from the guy whose roommate was an infamous serial killer."

"That why you moved to LA?" Anders's tone changed, and Trey wondered why.

"It was as far as I could go west in the US without hoping a six-hour plane ride over the Pacific or freezing my balls off in Alaska. It didn't matter in the end. One quick search of my name brought up all they needed to know about who I was. Luckily, I was able to snag a freelance position with the society pages to pay the bills."

"How did you know something was off about Gary?" Anders asked, his eyes lit with curiosity.

Well, at least the detective looked interested now instead of bored. "When I first moved in, Gary was quiet, but there was nothing specific I could put my finger on. It was more of a gut feeling. About a month in, he made a big deal about installing a padlock onto the outside of his bedroom door."

"A big deal?"

"Yeah, he'd shut the door and look over at me if I happened to be in the living room, before putting the padlock in place and locking it. Then he'd give it a few tugs to make sure it was set. He never came out and accused me of being in his room or stealing from him, but Gary made sure I knew the area was off-limits."

"I bet that was like waving a red cape in front of a raging bull," Anders said with a smirk.

"Damn straight it did. What was Gary hiding in there? We were sharing space and knew nothing about each other. He could have been the next Unabomber for all I knew."

"Of course."

"You gotta admit it would have made you curious too. Aren't you guys all about uncovering mysteries and finding truths?" The last thing a detective should be lecturing him about was curiosity.

Anders raised his brows and nodded, but didn't exactly answer.

"This went on for months. Every day, like a ritual or something. The moment he stepped out of his room, he locked it tight behind him. Wait, did I mention Gary was cheap?"

"What? No," Anders answered as his brows drew tight. The man could never hide what he felt. His face gave him away so quickly.

"Well, he is, and that's why picking the padlock was fairly easy. It had only three-pins to align for the barrel to rotate. Every time he'd shake that lock, I could barely contain myself from telling him it was a piece of junk metal. In the end, I'm glad I didn't because I have only rudimentary lock-picking skills."

"Do I even bother to ask why you know how to pick a lock?" Anders asked, rubbing his forehead.

"No." He wanted to smile. Frustrating the detective was too easy. "As I said, this went on for months until one evening when Gary was out having dinner with his mother. I took my chance. I could always relock it after I had a look around, and Gary would be none the wiser." In theory, it had seemed so simple and straightforward.

Trey stopped and took a deep breath to steady himself for what came next. "What I found when I opened that door, I could never lock away again. I called the police instead. Um... the smell was... There were pictures, and stuff from the women he killed. Some while they were still alive, others where he was taking selfies with their bodies. He had pieces of women's clothing hanging from a corkboard covered in these pictures. On the fucked-up shrine he'd built underneath, along with the burned candles, was a line of severed, decomposing fingers from his victims. The police called them trophies."

When he stopped recounting the events that would forever change his life, Trey's body shook, and unexpectedly, he found himself wrapped in a pair of strong arms. Sniffling, Trey hadn't realized that he'd been crying. When had that happened? He didn't cry over shit. Not anymore.

Then he heard movement to his right, and he'd quickly pulled away, fearing the worst. "Easy. Easy Trey, You're safe." Anders's voice reverberated through his body. "Miguel is here to check on you. Nothing to fear."

When Anders stood and moved away from the bed, Trey dried his eyes before looking over at Miguel, who was busy checking his machines. Anders returned to his desk without looking back as if nothing had happened.

Trey found himself alone once again, wishing he could be that cold and unfeeling. He pulled his blankets up tight to his chin and closed his eyes, shutting out the world around him.

Never let them see they hurt you.

***

Anders rolled over onto his back and stared at the metal fan blades rotating above him. He was having one hell of a time trying to get today's events cleared out of his head. He'd even tried meditation after watching a video online, but would never admit that to anybody. Still, he couldn't put the feeling of Trey in his arms out of his mind.

It wasn't only the touch. Anders had been busy shoring up his defenses for days. Keeping his distance was becoming increasingly difficult as Trey never complained and was always polite to everyone. The guy seemed to try to demand as little as possible even though he was still bed-bound and recovering from a second surgery for a gut wound.

Every day he fought his growing feelings for Trey. He wasn't the type of man the injured guy needed. Same old story, a career in law enforcement wasn't conducive to romantic entanglements. No guaranteed holidays off, unpredictable work hours, which often changed on the daily, and the danger of being injured every day on the job. It might be fun and exciting to fuck a cop, but commitment was a whole different ballgame. He didn't know how Ross and James pulled it off.

Christ, he needed Trey to do or say something selfish or mean soon so Anders could get his head back on straight. Instead, what does Trey do? He shared the unhealed emotional wounds of his past with strength and respect for how they changed his life. No inflated ego about how he was the one to stop the killings, or a lucrative book deal in the works to bring him fame and fortune. Anders somehow knew Trey would never capitalize on those poor women's deaths. Trey was honestly traumatized by what he'd seen, and all these years later, it still shook him.

Damnit. Anders growled before sitting up. He looked over at the monitor connected to a camera in Trey's room. Yep, creepy. But it was the best way to keep an eye on Trey. When his arm moved, Anders took a closer look to see his eyes were open. It seemed Trey was suffering from the same insomnia Anders was. After he learned how and what Trey had found in Gary's room, Anders had to wonder if Trey had slept a solid night since.

Anders ran his hands down his face before tearing away his blankets and throwing his legs over the side of the bed. Misery loves company, or so they say. Anders pulled on his gray t-shirt and shorts and headed for the door. The hub was quiet, and the restaurant and bar were closed. It was after two in the morning.

The hub had a full house. Miguel and Finn had moved in from their home in Pasadena so Miguel could take care of Trey.

Anders walked the few feet to Trey's closed door, and for the first time, he knocked instead of walking in without permission. When he heard a faint "come in," Anders opened the door and found Trey struggling to sit up as much as he could with his injury. The look of fear on his face threw Anders for a moment.

"What's wrong?" His voice was higher than usual.

"Nothing. Everything's okay," Anders assured while feeling like a heel for scaring the man.

Trey's shoulders drooped, and he let out a deep breath. "Then, why are you here this early in the morning?"

With each passing second, he was regretting his rash decision. "I saw you weren't sleeping, so I decided to come and check on you."

"Through your stalker camera," Trey chuckled as he pointed to the lens on the wall. "You couldn't sleep either?"

"No." That chuckle should not be making Anders feel almost giddy for Trey's levity. "I tried meditation." Shit, why did he tell him that?

"Meditation, you?" He laughed.

"Yeah, yeah. I was desperate, okay," Anders admitted.

"Well, come in and join the party," Trey said as he raised the head of his bed higher. "We could watch some television if you want."

"Sounds good," Anders replied. "Are you hungry? I could go scrounge us up some snacks."

"Chocolate?" Trey spoke right up. He'd have to remember that.

"I could check," Anders said, and added, "I could use a snack, myself."

"Okay. As long as you're already going. If you happen to come across any stray chocolate, I would love some," he said.

The hub had an open kitchen and living room area. The kitchen was basic: a fridge, stove, microwave, a couple of cupboards, and a single sink. Considering this area was only temporary, and a massive restaurant kitchen wasn't far away meant this kitchen was seldom used for meals.

A quick perusal of the cupboards produced a bag of barbeque chips and a couple of chocolate bars. He took one and then stopped by the fridge and picked up a couple of water bottles before turning to find that he was no longer alone in the room.

"Shit, Marian," Anders growled softly. "You surprised me."

"If that's all it takes, you might want to reconsider your vocation," Marian said as she passed him to get her own bottle of water from the fridge. "You hungry, detective?" she asked after looking over his supplies.

"It's for Trey and me. Neither of us could sleep, so we thought about watching a movie or something." Why did he feel like his mother had caught him?

"Ah, I see," she said with a peculiar smile and a nod. "Well, you two have a good night." She walked away, back down the hall.

"Okay." Yeah, he felt like a teenager doing something he wasn't supposed to be doing. "Goodnight."

Every time Anders thought he had a read on Marian, she went and did something that made him question what he'd figured out about her.

Shaking his head, he double-checked his haul and decided to grab another chocolate bar in case one wasn't enough. He would buy more tomorrow, but first, he'd have to find out which kind was Trey's favorite.

Anders stopped mid-stride.

What the hell was wrong with him? Favorite kind?. He'd get whatever Anders picked up. He'd be getting way too personal to know any of Trey's favorite things.

Anders would have to keep tighter control over his emotions.

Chapter Six

When Anders returned to Trey's room, the guy had everything ready for movie night. Well, movie at two fuckin' am. The television mounted on the wall was turned on. Trey's blankets were tidied and tucked around him, and he had the remote in his hand along with a hopeful expression on his face. Anders couldn't help but smile. *Shit.*

Raising the hand in which he held the chocolate bars, Anders said, "The hunt was victorious." *Seriously? What was wrong with him?*

"You laid siege to the kitchen and brought back the chocolate treasures you've pillaged. My hero." Trey responded without missing a beat. Why did that make Anders so damn happy?

"Skol," Anders cheered softly.

"Skol," Trey followed along.

He brought the snacks over and set them on the mattress beside Trey before moving the desk chair closer to the bed.

"What did you want to watch?" Trey asked.

"What are my options?" It'd been interesting to see if they could agree on something. Anders doubted they had the same taste in movies.

"There's a documentary on the dangers of fossil fuels, a cooking show where we can learn how to make pork pot-stickers, or an action movie franchise on late-night movie reruns."

For reasons he couldn't figure out, Anders didn't pick his favorite, and said without thinking. "What would you like to watch?"

Trey's head cocked to the side. "Well, that's a no-brainer. A good action movie wins every time."

Anders released a breath and said, "Thank god. We all know fossil fuels are bad, and I don't particularly like pot-stickers."

"You don't like pot-stickers?" Trey gasped in mock shock before smiling wide.

"Let's get this movie marathon on the road, smartass," Anders grumbled.

Trey laughed and changed the channel as an explosion flashed across the screen. That's what he was talking about.

Anders reached for the bag of chips at the same time Trey grabbed one of the chocolate bars. Their fingers touched and sent a spark through Anders that wasn't caused by static electricity.

Casually, he pulled his hand back, keeping a secure lock on his emotions and the bag of barbeque chips. He cleared his suddenly constricted throat and said, "Those were the only chocolate bars I could find. I'm not sure if you even like that type."

Trey looked down at the opened wrapper of candy and said, "All chocolate is good chocolate," before taking a big bite.

They both laughed, and Anders had to admit Trey was right. As the minutes passed, Anders relaxed and dug into his bag of chips. The sounds of gunfire and breaking glass filled the room even though the volume had been turned down low.

When the hero crawled into the ductwork, Anders couldn't help but shake his head. He'd been on burglary cases where some idiot decided to try the same thing and had to be cut free once he got himself stuck.

"I wonder how many people have tried that after this movie came out?" Trey asked, mirroring what Anders had been thinking.

"Too many," Anders answered. "From what I've been told, and what I've experienced, this form of stupidity continues to this day."

"How do they think, Gee, I'm two-hundred and fifty pounds, and that small space and thin piece of metal are going to hold me? Common sense says don't try it, but put it in a movie, and suddenly it's real and possible despite the law of physics."

"I know. It drives me crazy," Anders said. "The world would be better off if people used their common sense instead of blindly following along."

"Agreed." Trey reached for one of the bottles of water. He grunted and held on to his abdomen before he sat back without having reached the bottle.

"Here, I'll get it," Anders said before grabbing the water and handing it to Trey. "Are you in a lot of pain? Should I get Miguel?"

Trey smiled and said, "Not as much pain as I had a few weeks ago. I had Miguel lower the dose of my painkillers. Gotta titrate off that shit. I'm okay."

Anders turned in his chair to face Trey. "Why would you do that?" Trey's injury was severe, and he needed pain relief to heal. Anders didn't like to take medications unless necessary, but he knew when the brain was dealing with pain, the body took longer to heal.

"My mother lost her fight with drugs, and I don't want to tempt fate," Trey said.

Okay, there was a lot there to unpack, including Trey not looking at him when he spoke. Anders asked, "Your mom was addicted to pain killers?"

"Yeah." Trey kept his gaze glued to the TV. My father was killed in action halfway around the world when I was a baby. It's how she dealt with the loss."

"I'm sorry. To lose both parents had to be tough." Actually, it sucked. He'd been dealt a shit hand.

"She held out until I was eighteen before sending herself to be with my dad," Trey said. "There's that. In the end, I'd kept her grounded and from reuniting with my father in the afterlife. If there's such a thing."

Fuck. What would it do to a child knowing their remaining parent was biding her time before leaving him? Trey had been screwed over right from the start. Then add in a serial killer who still haunts Trey every day, and whose affiliation affected his opportunities to move ahead with his life. Life really did deal Trey a shit hand. The same killer was hunting him now.

"Gotta say, picking yourself up and moving forward with all that's happened is remarkable, man." For real, Anders doubted he'd be able to do the same if he'd been put in those situations, especially with the background Trey had. And the dude was working to save as many women and children as he could. Commendable barely scratched the surface.

Trey turned and looked him in the eyes. "I refuse to give up like my mother did."

Anders stared into those troubled dark eyes. He'd fucked up. He'd misjudged Trey. Made assumptions based on his own bias. Maybe he was a Viking asshole. A soft knock on the door forced Anders to climb out of the rabbit hole he was traveling down.

Miguel entered, and with a nod, he walked over to Trey's three machines, picked up his tablet, and began taking Trey's vitals, as he had four hours ago. The guy wasn't getting much sleep. He wrapped a cuff around Trey's upper arm and checked his blood pressure as Anders turned back toward the TV.

"Would you like to stay and watch the movie with us, Miguel?" Trey asked as the big man laid the tablet down. "I have another chocolate bar."

At first, Anders didn't think Miguel was going to answer, but he turned to Trey and said, "Maybe next time. Finn will worry."

Trey looked surprised, but said, "Okay. Next time."

Miguel left, and Trey looked over at him. "Six words. He finally spoke to me, right. I didn't hallucinate that."

"No, he spoke to you." Anders couldn't help but laugh.

He looked so pleased. "I knew I could wear him down with my winning personality."

"Never doubted you for a minute."

"That's a flat-out lie," Trey burst out laughing while holding onto his stomach. "You've doubted everything I've ever done since before you met me."

Anders felt his face heat. Shit. He didn't get flushed, but it was like Trey had read his thoughts. "Yeah, yeah. Moving forward."

"Okay, detective. Moving forward, I'd prefer to be given the benefit of the doubt." Trey raised a brow, and his wide eyes demanded an answer.

"You got it." Anders could do that.

"Deal."

"Deal."

***

"You have a family?" Trey asked while leaning back against his pillows. He was enjoying the time he and Anders were spending together. Gone was the tension and stress, which usually accompanied their discussions. It was a welcome change.

"Yeah. Mother, father, and two sisters. They live in Oslo, Norway," Anders answered before gulping his water.

"Are you close to them?"

"Yeah. Really close." He smiled as he answered. "I try to get back there as much as possible, but it's hard to find the time."

"You must get killer air miles." Trey chuckled. "What made you want to come to the United States to be a detective?"

"My family had been living here since I was a small child. My father relocated the family for a promotion. A year after I graduated from the police academy, my parents decided they wanted to slow down and return to Norway before retiring. My sisters decided to go with."

"You're the only one to stay?" Trey's stomach fell at the thought. He never knew his father, and his mother had checked out long before she'd died. By the sound of it, Anders had a good and loving family. Letting them go had to be difficult. Sure, Trey losing his mother sucked, but he thought it'd been worse watching her kill herself in pieces every day of his life.

"Yeah." One word belying a host of emotions.

"That had to make you lonely. I get it. I'm glad you still get to see them." Why it mattered, Trey didn't know, but he'd been beyond curious about Anders's life. "Do you have a wife or girlfriend waiting for you back in New York?"

"Nope. No boyfriend or husband to speak of. No time," Anders answered without skipping a beat. Out and proud. Nice.

"I know what you mean. The last date I had lasted all of ten minutes." It'd been a shit-show from the start.

"Ten minutes?" Anders tilted his head as his brows went up.

"The moment he disparaged the waitress, I was out of there. The guy commented on everything from the dark roots in her hair to her service speed and weight. I didn't leave before approaching the manager in case that asshole tried to complain about the waitress after I'd left. I never understood why some people need to belittle others to feel good about themselves." Trey had had some choice words for the bully, and the entire restaurant had heard them.

Anders nodded, and a thoughtful expression crossed his face. Trey hoped he hadn't dug up a painful memory for Anders by talking about his family and lack of companionship. "My bad, man. I didn't mean to cause you to relive anything painful."

Anders looked over at him and said, "I know you didn't. I miss my family at the oddest of times."

"Oddest?"

"Yeah, like when I'm on a case and need an ear to talk things over with. Every time I have to stop and consider what time it is in Norway," Anders explained.

"What time is it in Oslo now?" He wondered.

Anders looked down at his thick metal watch. "When I'm on the east coast, they are six hours ahead of me. In LA, it's nine hours."

"Wow, so it's around eleven in the morning. That would make it hard to call your family off the cuff when you felt like it," Trey said as he looked back from his clock on the bedside table. "You're having lunch when they're settling in for the night."

"Yep. I used to take my sisters to the Ranger's home games. I miss hanging out with them at a hockey game and heckling the visiting team," Anders said with a devilish look on his face. "We're hockey fans, and they're hurting in Norway. You'd think with all that ice, it'd be a big sport, but it's not. When we talk, I rub it in."

"Maybe we could go sometime. I'm good with heckling." *Where did that come from?* It was out of his mouth before Trey had even thought about it. He wanted to cheer up Anders, not invite himself to a hockey game.

Before Trey could think to take his words back, Anders said, "Deal. We'll make plans. I've never been to a game on the west coast before. Seems like a weird sport for a town full of palm trees."

Trey chuckled. He'd thought of that too when he moved here. Sighing, he was amazed at how fast he could go from wide-awake to barely keeping his eyes open. His body was tired, and he could almost feel it working to heal itself.

He'd enjoyed his time with Anders, and didn't want it to end, so he fought the sleep pushing down on him.

"You're getting tired," Anders said. "I should go."

"No, I'm having a good time," Trey argued.

"So am I, but you need your rest. How about we continue this tomorrow night starting earlier?" Anders looked hopeful.

"I'm in," Trey said before yawning.

"Here, let me get this." Anders picked up the water bottles and the candy wrapper. "I'll leave this here in case you wake up with a chocolate craving." He set the second chocolate bar on Trey's bedside table along with his water.

"Put it back in case someone wants it with their breakfast. I don't know, to make hot chocolate or something."

Anders smiled, and Trey wondered why. "I'm picking up some more tomorrow when I'm out, so don't worry." He moved his chair back behind the desk and headed for the door, but he stopped and turned to look at Trey. "I know you said all chocolate's good chocolate, but what's your favorite type?"

"Anything with peanuts in it." Trey was surprised the detective had asked.

"Get some sleep. See you tomorrow."

"Considering it's already tomorrow morning, I'll see you later." Why was he being cheeky?

Anders chuckled and nodded. "Yeah, today. Sleep well."

"You too."

Trey found himself staring at the door, wondering what had just happened. Were they friends now? Or would Anders go back to the cold, uncaring way he typically treated him?

God, he hoped not. That would suck.

Chapter Seven

Anders had brought Trey every type of chocolate bar available with peanuts. It was insane. He'd never eat that much in a month, let alone after a week when Anders had asked if he needed more.

Over that same week, Anders had shared even more information on the manhunt for Trey's former roommate. Including the identity of the woman who'd been connected to the finger, he'd found in the box. Her body had been discovered in a dumpster in China Town not far from Dodger Stadium. Her name had been Kelly, and she was a student at UCLA.

Her family and friends held a vigil on campus a few days ago. Trey had read the news and saw the pictures online. Like the one of Kelly's mother collapsed on the ground beside a tower of flowers built in her daughter's honor. If that didn't drive home Trey was a danger, nothing else would. He shared the blame, and it was gutting him. If given the choice, he'd take her place in a hot second if it meant Kelly would be alive today. She'd probably be in class right now, or laughing with her friends. *Fuckin' Olsen.*

Trey had felt guilty when he discovered he was a serial killer's roommate. This time it was worse since he knew Gary was killing women to get to him.

Sadly, she wasn't the only body to turn up missing a finger in the same timeframe. The longer it took to find the killer, the more guilt Trey felt. It didn't matter where he lived. Once Gary found him, the women in the area would be vulnerable. After five years in prison, Gary had to be enjoying his killing spree with relish. And yeah, while Trey had nothing to do with Gary escaping, Trey felt responsible.

The truth was wherever he went, Trey would be a danger to all the women who lived near him.

Knowing this, made his decision to leave easier. He'd been a magnet for bad luck for as long as he could remember, and he sure as hell wouldn't subject the people who were living in The Gates to Gary's madness. For a brief moment, Trey felt like he might've made friends. Enjoyed a small slice of normal. He should've known better.

Even with Rachel, Trey kept his distance. He visited the shelter only when necessary, choosing to send money rather than delivering it.

Today Miguel removed the last of the machines to which Trey had been hooked up. As each had been removed, one by one, he felt his constant companions over the last month were marching out after doing their job. He was far from healed, but he was out of the woods, which made it possible for him to get far away from The Gates crew before he got any of them killed.

Certain the psycho would follow him to the ends of the earth, Trey would have to pick a remote location, so Gary's only option would be to confront him. And he'd be ready. He owned a gun, and he would take the first opportunity he had to wipe Gary Olsen out of existence, at any cost. He'd put an end to the bastard's second killing spree, which could go on for years. Gary was adept at staying hidden, especially since he became a fugitive. There was no rehabilitation in the world capable of controlling and containing Gary's evil. Trey figured if tax dollars had to be spent to house someone in prison, he'd be a better choice than Gary Olsen.

Alone in his room, it was the perfect time for a test of his strength and abilities. Carefully, he edged his body closer to the left side of the bed. The cool sheets eased his way. With more strength than he thought he had, he managed to get his left leg over the side. His pain level was increasing, but he refused to stop. The quicker he was up on his feet, the sooner he could lead Gary away from a populated area.

After taking a moment to rest, Trey wiped his damp forehead and dragged his right leg over to join his left. Now he was sitting up, legs over the side of the bed, ready to go, but he wasn't moving. This was the first time his legs were lower than his body in over a month, and damn, damn, damn, they ached and throbbed something fierce.

He struggled to push past his fear of falling and ripping open his sutures and continued to inch forward. The tips of his toes were mere inches away from the wood floor when his bubble burst.

"What are you doing?" A loud, booming voice made him freeze in place. Miguel.

"What happened to knocking?" Trey tried to deflect.

"It's in the same place where my *remain in bed* must be located," he growled back.

Miguel had him there. "I know what you said, but you don't understand."

"Try me," Miguel grunted as he came over to the side of Trey's bed and lifted his legs back onto the mattress before covering him. "You'd be surprised by what I can understand."

Trey thought about it and decided Miguel might, in fact, get what Trey was trying to do. Marines were notorious frontline military who risked their lives saving other people all the time. From what Trey was able to glean from Miguel's behavior and demeanor, this guy was tougher than most.

"I have to go," Trey said in a rush.

"To the toilet?" Miguel asked. Trey had a catheter until a few hours ago. Miguel's scrunched brows were understandable.

Trey went with the truth. "No. Away from here. The Gates and everyone in it." He had trouble getting out the painful words. He figured this would be as close as Trey got to a family. Ever.

"Why?" Miguel's expression darkened. "As far as I know, you've been treated well."

"Of course I have. I'm grateful for the time I got to spend here, but I need to get stronger now that I'm machine-free so I can lead Gary away from here. It's me he's fixated on. It makes sense I shouldn't stay here much longer, or that psycho will begin targeting the people that live and work here." Miguel had to understand where Trey was coming from.

"You want to leave to save the rest of us?" Miguel's brows furrowed deeper into one big, black caterpillar.

"Ah, yeah."

Miguel shook his head as if Trey were a kid who wasn't processing what his father was telling him. "Are you insane?"

"No. But I will be soon with all the shit that keeps happening," Trey snapped. And there it was: a slight uptick in the one corner of

Miguel's mouth. "Of all people, I thought you'd understand, and help me to make it happen."

"You thought I'd help you commit suicide?" Miguel dropped his chin for a moment before lasering his gaze on Trey.

"No. Don't be dramatic. To begin with, I was hoping you could help me get stronger to stay awake longer than three hours. The further I can lead Gary away to a remote location, the better. C'mon. It's not like you can't see why I have to do this. You're a tactician. You know if the threat is removed from an area, you don't have to spread your resources thin protecting a large patch. LA county. Millions of people. The middle of the desert. Lizards and cactus. This isn't rocket science."

Miguel crossed his arms over his considerable chest. "Okay, Patton. What do you intend to do after you lead Gary away to where? The desert?"

"I'll wait for him to come for me," Trey tried to sound confident, though he was anything but. "Then I'll shoot that monster right between his eyes." He wasn't callous about human life, but Gary's continued existence was a threat to others.

"Shoot, who?" Anders's voice came from the open doorway.

"Does anyone knock anymore?" Trey huffed before laying back against his pile of pillows.

"Your *charge* wants to go out on a suicide mission," Miguel stated. "Thinks he can take Gary on alone."

"Rat."

"Pest," Miguel replied before exiting the room, leaving Anders standing in the doorway glaring.

He shut the door and said, "Want to tell me what that was all about?"

"No, but I'm guessing it isn't one of my options," Trey countered.

"Correct, it's not," Anders said as he stood with his hands on his hips. "Let's hear it. What are you up to now?"

Trey huffed and crossed his arms over his chest and was sure he didn't look as intimidating as Miguel, which sucked. "I thought you were going to give me the benefit of the doubt from now on?" Trey grasped at straws to avoid telling him the plan since he was positive Anders wouldn't go for it.

"There's the benefit of the doubt and facts. The word shoot came out of your mouth. That's a fact. Now spill it."

Trey knew there was no way out of this, so he'd do his best to make Anders see reason, even if Miguel refused to.

"You have to agree that Gary is in LA because of me."

"Where are you going with this?"

"You wanted facts. Let's do facts."

Anders's eyes narrowed, but he remained silent as he moved his chair closer to Trey, turned it around, and sat with his arms draped over the back of the chair.

"Fact number one: Gary followed me here. I have no idea how he found me, but he's here, and innocent women are dying. Fact two: That psycho will continue killing until he's either found or kidnapped me. Fact three: No one has seen him, and Gary's not leaving willingly without me."

"Agreed," Anders growled, but didn't dispute the facts.

"Fact four: I can lead him away to a remote place, and as you overheard me say earlier, shoot him and end his psychotic rampage once and for all." There, the facts.

Anders stood up so fast from his chair it fell and bounced on the floor. "Not a chance. You in a hurry to die?"

"Listen, it makes sense. What is one life worth compared to so many innocent people?"

"You're an innocent person," Anders countered. "I can't believe you'd offer yourself up on a silver platter."

"Seriously, this life of mine isn't all it's cracked up to be," Trey huffed. "This plan is the best solution to an impossible situation. Hell. It's not like I have a family or a circle of friends who'll miss me. The only thing I'd regret leaving behind is the shelter, but I have life insurance, and the shelter is the beneficiary. When the policy pays out, they'll be better off than they are currently. Not pity, only the facts, detective."

"I will," Anders growled as he ran his fingers through his blond hair.

Excuse me? I didn't hear him right. "You'd miss me? Up until this week, you could barely stand to be in the same room as me."

"I was wrong about you," Anders admitted.

"Can I get that in writing?" Trey had no idea why he was joking at a time like this. Stress did funny things to people.

Anders carried on as if Trey hadn't said a word. "I pictured you as a smarmy journalist who ran a PI gig on the side and was willing to destroy lives for a quick buck."

"Wow, tell me what you really think." That hurt, but it wasn't a surprise. "There are those out to make a quick buck and are willing to do anything to get it, but it's not all of us. The same as not all detectives take bribes."

Anders shook his head. "Yeah, well, I thought that before I got to know you," Anders huffed. "You're not what I expected, and I've never taken a bribe in my life."

"I could be playing nice," Trey argued. "I'm in a pretty vulnerable situation and aware this is the best way to assure your continued help."

"Nice try," Anders said as he bent to pick up his chair. "You're not taking off on some deluded mission to sacrifice yourself for the greater good."

"Who's going to stop me?" Trey raised his chin in challenge.

Trey had expected Anders to lay down the law, but what he hadn't expected was for his bedroom door to fly open and for Finn, Sawyer, Marian, Saint, Joey, and more Gates staff and their partners to walk in with scowls on their faces.

"Ask the question again," Sawyer said as he leaned forward.

"News travels fast around here. Gossip much?"

"Face it. You have people who care about you," Anders stated. "In answer to your question, all of us will stop you from taking on a serial killer alone."

Trey felt a little dizzy, and slightly nauseous. He chalked it up to trying to get out of bed, not being able to keep down solid food, and having a room full of people staring at him with pissed-off expressions. What did they expect? Hell, his mother had checked out on him long before she died. He was a pariah because he'd been Gary's roommate, and now he was the cause of at least two deaths.

It wasn't until he wiped away the hot tears running down his face Trey pinpointed the main source of his riotous emotions. He'd gone from being alone in this world to having an unusual group of people who'd adopted him.

A sense of belonging swamped him as he looked over at the handsome detective who'd been the catalyst for his new existence.

Chapter Eight

The damn building was close to being a fortress, but there was always a way in if he looked hard enough. Gary had proven that time and again. Once he got his hands on his old roommate, he could move his show on the road. A state-by-state road trip. He'd always wanted to see America.

He shuffled to the back of the commercial van he'd hotwired outside Nevada. He enjoyed watching his prey from behind the darkly tinted windows. No need to hide himself behind the pleasant expression he wore to entice his victims closer.

It could have been his well-practiced smile or his golden hair—a gift from his mother—but they always came to him. The moment he thought of her, Gary growled and clenched his teeth in rage. The traitor had turned her back on him, her son, and he'd never forget or forgive her betrayal. One day Rachel, that back-stabbing bitch would pay for her lack of loyalty. Getting caught was all her fault. He never wanted a roommate, but *she* made it a requirement for him to receive his monthly allowance. Something about being antisocial.

He'd learned a lot of new skills behind bars in preparation for this mission, and he intended to use them all. If he couldn't get inside the stone fortress, Gary would make Trey come out. Simple math. Trey plus one of the idiots who worked at The Gates, equaled a life for a life trade. He was having a hard time choosing which one of them would be enough incentive. Who would cause Trey the most pain?

That little shit thought he could walk away and live the happy-happy after destroying his life. He had locked his door, but the bastard still managed to get inside. He should have gone with his gut and gotten rid of Trey before the idiot got the chance to stop him.

None of that mattered now. All that remained was to make Trey pay for ruining his mission. The voices were quiet now, but it wouldn't last long. It never did, and then he'd be forced to hunt again to gain a respite from their constant demands.

Using the tip of his boot, he pushed the limp, pale arm back under the faded, torn tarp. He had to find a place to drop off his cargo before his hunt began anew tomorrow.

In a couple of days, he'd find a new vehicle, maybe even something with that Californian vibe. A sunroof sounded about right. He'd never be able to continue his work using a convertible unless he found the perfect location to provide him with the privacy he needed.

"Candy apple red." His voice cracked from disuse, and the iron taste in his mouth confirmed his split lip had reopened. He didn't remember the women he'd picked up years ago being as strong as these last few. In the end, it still hadn't stopped him from his mission.

They didn't matter. None of his sacrifices did. Trey's end would come, and once Gary had his revenge, and the feel of Trey's slim neck between his hands had become a thing of the past, nothing would stop him. The world may have been shocked by the likes of Bundy, Dahmer, and the Night Stalker, but they hadn't seen anything yet.

Gary took a passing glance at the lifeless body lying on the floor of the van and removed his Bowie knife from his ankle holster.

Soon.

Very soon.

Chapter Nine

Another body had turned up much closer to The Gates and had alarm bells blaring inside of Anders's head. Olsen had found out where Trey was. No way dumping a body here was a coincidence. The bastard was leaving them like calling cards all over DTLA, but each time a new body turned up, they were found closer to The Gates than the time before.

Anders wouldn't leave Trey's side, but at times he wished he could go out there and hunt down the killer, and lock him so deep inside a penitentiary he'd never have the chance to escape again.

It had been over a week since Trey announced his intention to lead Olsen away from DTLA, and as he continued to grow stronger it worried Anders the stupid idiot might go through with it. Miguel had begun teaching Trey how to defend himself, including the places on the human body where he could hit or jab to incapacitate a person so he could make a getaway. Useful information, but Anders wasn't leaving Trey to his own devices to take on Gary no matter how much training he had.

Yeah, he'd grown attached to the guy, and didn't want him risking his life on a suicide mission. Weeks ago, Anders had lost his fight to keep Trey at arm's length, and he'd have to deal with the fallout if things went to hell because of it.

In the meantime, all the LEOs involved in the case kept circling while asking what was it going to take to catch this killer? Every possible agency was involved. The FBI, The US Marshalls Office, NYPD, LAPD, and the LA county sheriff's office. Other state police forces were all notified and were provided with daily updates as the body count crept up.

The media was having a field day with the murders, and had dragged up everything from the old New York case and trial from years ago. Gary's image continued to be splashed across every screen, large and small in various news stories, and from the LAPD asking people to call the police if they saw anyone matching his description.

They had nothing.

Anders adjusted the projector screen to line up with the square table. Two place settings had been properly arranged with all the trimmings, including a bottle of sparkling grape juice. He didn't have a clue about proper table setting, so he'd left that up to Joey, Marian, and Bradley, while Alexander prepared the meal.

Anders hoped Trey enjoyed his surprise. It seemed the stronger Trey became physically, the worse he felt emotionally. He blamed himself for everything that was happening, no matter what anyone tried to tell him.

On Monday nights, Saint shut down the restaurant a few hours earlier than their normal closing time. Anders and Trey had continued their ritual of movie watching in the evenings, and he'd decided to spice it up in his mission to make Trey happy. Even if it was only temporary.

As if thinking of him made the man appear, Trey came walking into the closed restaurant with Finn by his side. His adorable look of confusion was easy to spot. Anders pulled back one of the chairs at the table and held out his hand, indicating Trey should sit.

"What's going on?" Trey asked, his eyes wide as his gaze darted from side to side. "I've never been in here before."

"Come sit down and rest. That's the furthest you've walked since you started your physical therapy," Anders stated, not wanting him to overdo it his first time out of the hub.

Trey looked at Finn and asked. "Where are all the people?"

"We're closed," Finn answered while leading him to the chair. "This," he tilted his chin to the table, "was all set up by Anders for you."

Trey turned to look at him, and Anders felt compelled to answer his unasked question. "This is movie night with pizzazz."

"Pizzazz?" Trey's smile widened. "Did you just use the word pizzazz, detective?"

Anders nodded. "Yeah. Now sit your ass down."

Trey chuckled and eased himself onto the thick cushion. Instead of shuffling him closer to the table, Anders moved the table closer to

Trey. The less jarring, the better. Anders didn't want to cause Trey any unnecessary pain. He'd had plenty of that in his life.

"What's the plan?" Trey asked, a spark of excitement in his eyes.

"A great dinner and a movie on the big screen," he answered before pointing toward the roll-up screen. "Don't worry if you get tired. We'll take the movie back to your room and finish it there."

"Sounds like you've thought of everything," Trey said as he looked around and pointed at the bottle buried in the ice bucket. "I don't think I should have alcohol given my liver situation."

Anders reached down and lifted the bottle for Trey to read the label. "Agreed, that's why this is sparkling grape juice."

"Good thinking. We'll save the portion of my organ I have left and wait to drink alcohol until I'm fully healed." Trey rubbed his abdomen as he spoke. There were still more than a few big bandages under his shirt.

"For dinner, we have a protein-rich meal to help you along with your recovery. Baked salmon in a pureed sweet potato and shrimp reduction over a bed of white rice. How's that sound?"

"Amazing," Trey looked shocked. "I've never had a fancy dinner in a place like this."

"Place like this?" Anders asked, unsure what he meant by that.

"Yeah. High-end furnishings and period pieces, lush velvets, flower arrangements, chandeliers, real dark wood, and brass. The works." Trey's head kept turning like it was on a swivel stick. "Do you think we can have a look around the restaurant and lounge before I have to go back to my room?"

"Of course. You're not a prisoner here. With the place closed, there's no chance of Gary getting near you. Besides, Miguel brought an old friend in for added security. You'll meet him tomorrow."

"More security?"

"Yeah. Gary should be getting anxious right about now, and is likely to do something desperate to get to you," Anders explained. "Now, let's get our dinner and a movie on the road."

Trey's thoughtful expression changed as he smiled wide and nodded. "Cool. This is so exciting. I'm more of a *eat alone at a diner* kinda guy."

Anders's heart couldn't help but melt. The more he learned about Trey, the further away his mind moved from all the preconceived notions he'd held.

Marian appeared out of the back carrying a large tray, and when Anders rose to help her, she snapped at him to sit back down. Bradley came out behind her, carrying one of those small foldable tables for Marian to set the tray on.

Trey looked ready to explode with excitement. Anders would have to remember to do this more often. His mind screeched to a halt. He was making more mental plans with Trey and waited for his usual panic to set in. When it didn't, he had his answer.

"Oh my god, everything looks so beautiful," Trey gushed while looking at the spread of food being set on the table. "Thank you. Everything looks delicious. Please tell Alexander and everyone who helped him. I'll never forget this."

Marian and Bradley smiled as they went about placing their plates in front of them. Finn reached for the sparkling grape juice and unscrewed the cap. Not nearly as elegant as a corkscrew, but it would do the trick. After he filled their glasses and Marian had taken the empty tray away, the lights were dimmed, and the movie began.

They'd always liked watching television while they were eating, and Anders acted like this was no different. This setup was comfortable, and he liked it. When the movie's theme music began playing, Trey's head popped up like he had a spring in his neck.

"You didn't?" Trey gasped.

"You mentioned that you like rom-coms. I thought this went well with the ambiance." Anders couldn't keep the grin from his face.

As the skyline of Seattle moved across the screen, Trey's eyes lit up. "I said it in passing, but you remembered."

Anders wasn't sure what to say, so he took a bite of the perfectly cooked salmon. The flavors and juices burst in his mouth with his first bite, making Anders moan his appreciation. "Alexander is a god with food."

Trey took a bite, and moaned as well. His moan did interesting things to Anders's body. Things it would take a few minutes to return to its "resting" position.

"This is so tender and delicious. There's a sweet flavor to it with the subtle hints of citrus. I've heard Alexander was a famous chef back east, and I can see why. I believe cooking is an art. One you can experience through all five senses."

Anders nodded, but refrained from talking while taking another bite. After that, they both dug into their dinners and eventually began chatting and watching their movie. Except for his family, Anders had never felt more contented in his life than he did right here with Trey.

***

They'd finished their delicious dinners and paused the movie so he could have a look around The Gates's public areas. The closest he'd gotten to being inside before this was months ago when he'd been staking out the building and Miguel was guarding the entrance.

Trey couldn't keep his eyes on one thing long before another architectural feature caught his attention. The place was truly spectacular, with its floor-to-ceiling windows covered by rich velvet drapes. The Gates namesake gates were hung on the inside of the entrance on either side of the front door commanding respect as they towered above everything else. From their height and girth to the green inlaid carvings of the head and torso of a man, front legs of a horse, and a tail like a merman, the gates were unique, imposing, and hailed from Hollywood's golden age.

The sumptuous lounge brought back images of a time when women cut their hair in short bobs, and flappers danced the Charleston in their low waist, high hemline dresses. From the gold and red accents, to what looked to be the original wood-carved bar spanning the length of one wall, Trey was in awe.

Several carved panels were inlaid into the bar's front, but one had been hung on the wall behind the bar in a glass case. It was a stunning carving of a staircase rising into the clouds. Everywhere he looked, there was something more interesting than the last thing he'd noticed. This building was a treasure.

"It's like floating through history," Trey whispered. "Max's team did a wonderful job of restoring the original life into this building."

"Yeah. They've done the old building justice. Nothing was overlooked," Anders said while placing his hand under Trey's bent arm as he continued to lead him around.

Something had changed in Trey when it came to Anders Nilsen. No longer did he find the detective's constant hovering or endless questions annoying. Now he looked forward to the time they spent together, but he wondered if he was confused what with everything else that was happening around them, not to mention how groggy his recovery made him.

Even if what he felt was real, Anders would be gone the moment Gary was caught. A passing flirtation, which would lead to nothing. Anyway, Trey should be thinking about self-preservation instead of leaning closer to Anders to catch a scent of the spicy notes of his cologne.

There was something about Anders, which drew Trey like nothing before in his life. In this moment, he was happy and felt safe, two things he'd never been. Too bad it would soon end.

As they continued to walk, Trey was getting tired. Before he had a chance to mention it, Anders had them heading back to their movie, where they found a small couch sitting where their table used to be.

"Wow, I've never felt so cared for," Trey said aloud without thinking. "Ignore me. I'm gushing like an idiot."

Anders took hold of Trey's hand and helped him to sit. "You're no idiot."

On the small table in front of them sat two water glasses, a pot of coffee, cups, and chocolate heaven sitting on a plate. Chocolate cake covered by chocolate mousse, topped by a fantastic mini chocolate sculpture with gold leaf, chocolate drizzle, a sprinkle of peanuts, and cocoa powder.

"Did you ask for this? It's beautiful." It reminded him of an art piece.

"Well, you love chocolate, so I figured it would be something nice for you to snack on through the remainder of our movie," Anders said. "Here. Have some water."

"You even remembered the nuts." He took a deep breath and asked, "What gives, detective? Are we on some kind of date?"

"If you'd like it to be. I wanted to make you happy. I know how hard all this has been on you," Anders explained.

"Don't get me wrong. You've done a great job. I'm beyond happy, but why all the," he waved his hand at the table, "fuss?"

Anders didn't look ruffled by the questions. "Because I care about you."

Trey was done with second-guessing his every move. Considering he'd almost died, and had a killer on his trail, he didn't see the point in mincing words. "Care about me as someone you need to protect because of the case. As your friend, or romantically?"

Anders reached forward and grasped Trey's hand. "I care about this case and keeping you safe. I also care for you as a friend because you're a good person, and I care about you on a more personal level. Look, I know I behaved like a dick when we first met, and I'm sorry. I don't have a clue what I'm doing, or what's going to happen, but I'd like to see where this goes. If you're completely against trying, then I swear to protect you, and I won't treat you any differently than I would a good friend."

Well, Trey asked for honesty, and he got both barrels. "What about going back to New York once Gary is caught?"

"I'm open to change.

Was Trey? He'd been alone for a long time. Could he allow someone to get close, and could he trust it?

Then it hit him. Anders was already that close. Trey had shared things about himself with Anders he'd never told another living soul. He never fully trusted anyone, not even Rachel, but he trusted Anders.

Those pale blue eyes watched him while Anders waited for his answer.

I'd like to see where this goes as well," Trey said, feeling like a fumbling teenager.

Anders smile was instantaneous, and he leaned over and took Trey's lips in a gentle kiss. *To hell with that.* Trey reached up and took hold of the detective's shirt collar and dove in for a deep, tongue-filled kiss, which had them both moaning before they parted.

"Let's do that often," Anders suggested. The pupils of his eyes were blown so wide open Trey could barely make out the blue.

"Deal." Trey laughed, feeling lighter than he had in a long time. "Now, let's devour this chocolate piece of heaven."

"Deal."

Chapter Ten

Brick? The guy's name was Brick?

Where did Miguel find these guys? Was there an app somewhere he could download to order his former military members? To think Trey believed Miguel was scary. This Brick guy took the cake. Tall, tattooed, and terrifying, with muscles to spare and an expression, which made Trey wonder if this was some sort of punishment.

"Brick is a retired Navy Seal. We've crossed paths a time or two. He'll watch over you when I'm not around," Miguel explained.

"Are you leaving?" Trey asked. Where would he be going at a time like this?

"For a couple of days, but you'll be safe," Miguel assured. "Besides, Anders will be back this afternoon."

At the mention of his new boyfriend, Trey couldn't contain his smile as warmth raced through him. It had been a little over a week since their date night, and as of a few days ago, Anders had begun sleeping in Trey's bed overnight. They'd done nothing more than holding each other while they slept, but that was all right. He'd never felt so safe, warm, and cared for before. The intimacy was there without the sex, though Trey couldn't wait until his body was ready for more strenuous activity.

They'd spend hours talking about everything and nothing, memories from the past to hopes for the future. Stunts they'd pulled as teenagers, and stories about a time when the world felt safe. When sitting under a tree wasn't a waste of time.

"Wait, I finally get you to talk to me, and you're leaving. Back to silence, it is. And things were going so well."

"I'll have you know I'm an excellent conversationalist," Brick said. "Fluent in five languages, and three dialects."

Trey should've known better than to judge the guy by his looks. As it turned out, Brick could be friendly. Okay, maybe this won't turn out too badly.

"Whoa, you've picked up a few new ones, cowboy. You sure there's enough room in that thick skull of yours to hold it all?" Miguel smiled as he took a shot at Brick.

Brick laughed. "Don't worry, buddy. I'll pick up some crayons later today and explain it to you."

The two joked back and forth, and Trey had never seen Miguel smile so much, unless Finn, his husband, was around. It was a good look on him. It made Trey happy watching Miguel open up.

"Don't worry. I won't be far if you need me," Brick stated. "I've got more than a few juicy stories about this ground lover for you while he's gone."

"Great." This was sure to be entertaining. "Those I've got to hear."

"Wait a minute, that wasn't part of this deal," Miguel groaned, making Trey laugh, and reflexively hold his stomach, expecting the pain to come. When it didn't, he almost cheered.

"You okay, man?" Miguel asked.

"Yeah," Trey said. "I can finally laugh without much pain at all."

"That's good," Miguel said. "That wound has healed up nicely. Soon enough, you'll be up and walking around without a problem."

"What about our lessons?" Trey asked. He had an acute interest in self-defense for obvious reasons.

"Brick will continue to teach you while I'm gone," Miguel replied.

"Where are you going, anyway?" Trey asked, unable to stem his curiosity even though it was none of his business.

Miguel's expression changed as he said, "Hunting."

"You're going hunting? For what?"

"An animal that needs to be put down," Miguel answered. Before Trey could ask any more questions, the big guy said, "Everything is all set up. I shouldn't be long." Miguel headed to the door with Brick in tow but stopped when he was almost over the threshold. "You'll be safe here, so don't get any crazy ideas in your head about facing Gary alone." Then they were gone, and his door was shut behind them.

Trey sat staring at his laptop as he thought things through, and it hit him Miguel was probably joining the hunt for Gary. Now he was in danger because of Trey. When would it end? When would the fates decide Trey had paid enough? His anger raged inside him without relief.

Soon enough, he'd have no other choice but to face that monster again, and Trey would finally have his chance to end the reign of terror.

***

Trey rubbed his tired eyes. He'd been asleep for over three hours and still felt ready for another nap. He was able to get around on his own. Mostly. Unfortunately, it took a lot of his energy, but he'd refused help, except sometimes when he got in bed. He had to keep pushing. It was the only way to gain his strength back.

He slid his legs over to the edge of the mattress and slowly stood as straight as he could with his stomach still tender and healing. He waited impatiently for the few seconds of lightheadedness to pass before moving forward towards his bathroom. He flipped on the light switch and hissed as the stark light filled the room, burning his sore eyes.

It took him a few moments and several blinks to clear his vision and become used to the brightness, but he made it to the vanity and turned on the water. He looked up and caught a glimpse of himself in the mirror.

"Holy hell," he groaned as he reached for his toothbrush. He accepted he wasn't a cover model, a Navy Seal, or even the boy next door. Plain. Average. Easily forgettable.

His hair was sticking out in every direction, and his pale face highlighted the dark circles under his eyes. He looked and felt like crap. Glancing over at the walk-in shower, he knew what he needed to fix the problem.

Miguel had cleared him to take showers, so that's what he'd do.

After a bit of jostling, he managed to brush his teeth and was able to get out of his loose-fitting t-shirt, jogging pants, and underwear. Looking back into the mirror, he took a moment to examine the healing scar running from above his belly button to the top of his pubes. With his index finger, he traced the red puckered skin from his surgeries and the unmistakable circular scar left from the bullet.

He was no prize, but the scars seemed to put a finer point on it. He shook his head at being so concerned over his appearance when he was lucky to be alive.

"Want to take a shower?" Anders's deep voice made Trey jump and rush to cover himself with a towel.

"Seriously, dude. Knock," Trey growled, more out of shock than anything.

"I'm sorry," Anders said while walking closer to take Trey into his strong arms. "I should've thought I might startle you before coming in."

Nice sentiment. It wasn't a case of being territorial or feeling crowded by their new living arrangement: he'd never been naked in front of Anders before. Of course, parts of him had been exposed when he was confined to the hospital bed, but never full-on. He wrapped the towel tighter around himself.

"So?" Anders asked.

"So?" What?

"Do you want to have a shower?" Anders asked while pointing his thumb in its direction.

"Yeah. I was considering it," Trey said. "I need to wash away the grime covering me." Even though he'd had numerous bed baths when he was connected to the machines, he'd dreamed of the feeling of hot water pounding down on his sore neck. Now he was untethered. He took advantage of the heavenly feeling as often as he could.

Anders released him and reached into the large walk-in shower to turn on the water. "I'll get this nice and warm," he said and then did something Trey hadn't seen coming: Anders began to unbutton his shirt. All the blood from Trey's one head rushed to the other, leaving him dizzy all over again.

Oh my god.

It'd been some time since Trey had gotten naked with man, and by his body's response, it'd been too long. No matter what he tried to do, thinking of baseball, naming the elements on the periodic table, looking everywhere else except at the inches of hard flesh slowly being revealed, nothing worked to stop his dick from standing at attention and tenting the towel wrapped around him.

Anders slid out of his shirt and let it fall to the floor. Did the man know he was sex on a stick? Every inch of his *can I please touch it* skin seemed to glow with good health while defined muscles created hills and valleys Trey wanted to explore. In depth. Excellent gene pool in the Nilsen family. Anders unhooked his belt buckle and shucked his jeans in one quick motion until he stood before Trey in only his black boxer briefs.

"Ready?" he asked.

"For what?" Logic failed Trey.

Anders chuckled. "Your shower."

Steam filled the bathroom, obscuring the mirror and saving Trey from further comparisons between their physiques.

"You keeping your underwear on?" Trey asked as he looked down to find Anders's cock pushing for freedom from its confines. *Damn.*

"Yeah. You're too big of a temptation. It's better to have something between us," Anders said. "Your body is nowhere near ready for what I'd love to do with you."

"My body?" Trey asked while waving his finger over his abdomen while still holding tight to his towel like a lifeline.

Anders's answering grin and heated look had Trey's temperature rising, but he was confused. "I'm short and nothing special, especially now that I've been lying in bed and my muscles have been atrophying. Not to mention my new assortment of scars."

"You're what I want. As for the scars, I'm sorry you had to go through that pain. I wish I could take that away for you."

"Thanks. But, they're there for life." There was no making lemonade from this lemon. "Compared to you, I'm not even in the same state, let alone ballpark."

Anders moved closer and gathered Trey, towel and all, into his arms. "I'm attracted to all of you, top to bottom. You got those scars saving another person's life and risking your own. You're a pain in the ass, but you're my pain in the ass and I wouldn't change a thing."

Trey had never been told anything like that before. "That's how you really see me?"

"Yeah." Anders nodded. "I fought the attraction until I couldn't. Maybe not at first, but after I got to know you, I wanted you."

"Why?" What had held him back?

Anders took a few moments before saying, "How about we have our shower first. It'll make you feel better, and after, when I have you next to me in bed, I'll tell you the whole story?"

Trey sucked in a deep breath and let it out slowly. "Deal." He dropped his towel, walked into the steamy shower, and stood under the hot stream of water coming from the rainfall showerhead.

He could feel Anders walking in behind him, but kept his eyes closed, allowing the hot water to rush over him. It felt decadent and heavenly, and he couldn't fight back the moan escaping his lips. This was what he'd needed.

"Keep doing that, and you'll test my resolve," Anders chuckled.

"It feels so good," Trey responded before ducking out of the spray of water.

I'm sure it does. Now come here," Anders said while motioning with his soapy hands for Trey to come closer. God, he was beautiful, all wet and soapy.

It was no hardship for him to get up close to the handsome detective. Anders opened his arms wide, and Trey had no second thoughts before filling them.

"There you go," Anders crooned as he began rubbing the soapy cloth over his tingling skin. Anders's strong touch gentled when he went anywhere close to Trey's abdomen, making him relax even further. His rock-hard dick showed no sign of deflating, and Anders ignored it.

"Turn around," he said. "I'll wash your back and legs for you."

Trey turned, and firm fingers worked their magic as his body loosened up. As Anders washed him, he also rubbed sore muscles in Trey's neck, shoulders, and back. When he crouched down to continue with Trey's legs, he went from his lower back to his butt. Washing each cheek until his warm fingers slid across Trey's soapy skin, leaving him panting from the up close and personal attention he was receiving.

When Anders stood, he remained behind Trey, and though Anders wasn't flush against him, his long cock pressed into Trey's back. Anders reached around, and using his soapy hands, he began lathering Trey's throbbing balls and hard cock. He gave up trying to stifle his moans, and allowed them to have free reign.

"That's it, babe. Relax back into me. I'll give you what you need," Anders groaned.

The feel of Anders's large hands cupping Trey's balls while his other hand began a steady rhythm pumping up and down his aching hard-on was magnificent. Anders's lips began exploring Trey's shoulders and neck as quick nibbles were chased away by soft kisses and a nimble tongue.

"Lean back," he groaned even louder. "I'd never let you fall."

Trey believed him, and for the first time in his life, he had someone to catch him. The overwhelming feeling of complete trust was freeing as he leaned back into the amazing man.

Anders ran the palm of his hand over Trey's cock, lightly squeezing the mushroom head, and making Trey shudder. He didn't know how much more he could take without exploding into his lover's hand.

"I'm close. Feels so good. Please don't stop." Trey wasn't above begging for what he desperately needed.

"Not a chance of stopping."

The sound of splashing water, wet skin, and moans filled the shower as Anders began pumping his fist faster while the fingertips of his other hand circled Trey's hole. He dug his fingers into Anders's thick arms as his world began to spin. He was on the edge, but desperately needed something to push him over.

"Come," Ander commanded, his deep voice resonating through every cell of Trey's body.

He threw his head back and hollered his release to the walls and undoubtedly anyone within earshot. Trey couldn't find the will to be embarrassed as his legs gave out, and he was helped up by Anders's strong arms.

Before Trey could be embarrassed, Anders captured Trey's lips in a punishing kiss, which left him gasping for air. He felt like a warm noodle lounging back and closing his eyes as the rain shower cascaded over their bodies.

***

Trey was tucked in bed, wrapped in blankets and Anders's arms, which felt like steel around him. Damn. He'd fallen asleep.

"Shit. Did I pass out?" Trey asked.

Anders's deep chuckle was answer enough.

"Oh man, sorry. I'm not usually the fainting maiden type." Yep, his face was getting hot. What the hell was wrong with him? *Man up right now.*

Anders propped his head on Trey's shoulder. "Sorry for what?"

"Leaving you hanging like that. I'm not a selfish lover, I promise." Sure, Trey got what he needed when he was with a lover, but never at the other guy's expense.

Anders pushed up closer and gently turned Trey onto his back so that they were almost nose to nose. "You are the least selfish person I know. No one is keeping count, least of all me. We make love when and how we want to. There's no challenge between us. I wanted to give you pleasure, and believe me, I got a lot of pleasure from watching you get off. It was powerful and addictive."

Powerful and addictive, not two words Trey imagined would be used in the same sentence as it related to him. "Me?"

"Yeah, you. Now close your eyes, and get some more rest. It's the best thing to do for your recovery," Anders instructed while laying his head down on the pillow beside Trey.

"Hold on a minute. I believe you owe me an explanation." No way would he forget.

"Explanation?" Anders asked, but his smile gave him away.

"Don't give me that bullshit. You were going to explain why you kept your distance," Trey responded.

"Oh, that explanation," he joked while pulling Trey closer. "I remember."

"Was it the fact that I'm a journalist for the society pages or that I'm a scuzzy PI reporting on affairs in dark alleys? Wait, maybe it's because I'm cursed."

"Wait, what? Cursed?" Anders right eyebrow shot upwards.

Chapter Eleven

Anders wasn't sure he heard right. Cursed was a harsh word to describe yourself and your life, though he had to admit, Trey had been put through the wringer.

Of all things he'd expected him to say, that was not it. Trey believed Anders was steering clear of getting close because of Trey's past. There was no way he'd allow him to continue to believe that.

The guilt he carried was unimaginable, and Anders was only scraping the surface. How had he survived and kept it together was a testament to his strength and resilience. It made Anders want to wrap up Trey and protect him from the world.

"You were never the cause." Let's get that straight. "I admit, at first I used your career and history as an excuse, but the reality is I was a coward. Straight up."

"Coward? You're no coward." Trey stated, making Anders smile.

"Defending my honor?" Anders teased. "Dear knight."

"Somebody has to, knucklehead."

"In this instance though, I was a coward." He could admit that. "This goes way back to when I first started out on the force. I was naïve. I think we all are to some extent when we graduate from the academy. Taking everything into yourself, the happy, the sad, and the crazy ugly. I let it affect me emotionally. You know the saying, the road to hell is paved with good intentions," Trey nodded. "Well, the deaths, the pain, the never-ending suffering, the systemic injustices, and the things I saw and did began to wear me down, and took a physical toll, but I kept going because I swore to protect and serve. It wasn't until my family approached me with their concerns that I realized what I was doing. I'd changed so much they worried I'd burn out fast, and I wouldn't come back from it."

"I never stopped to think about what you must go through on a daily basis," Trey admitted. "It can't be easy being a cop, especially in a big, complicated city like New York."

"Too true." He sighed. "When I moved over to my new unit after becoming a detective, I took a hard look at myself and decided to make changes. I decided I couldn't get close to any of the people involved in my cases anymore, no matter how heart-wrenching or messed up they were. There was a particular case that was the catalyst for the change."

"I believe it. There's always a moment in your life that's been burned into you and brands you forever," Trey said. "Mine was when I'd received yet another rejection in trying to break into a career in serious journalism. I decided then and there I didn't give a shit what anyone thought about me or my past. I'd take any job no matter what people might say about my character, as long as it was legal."

Anders leaned down and kissed this man with a kind heart who understood what he felt. "That's it. Like something snaps inside of you."

"Yeah. You can almost hear it breaking in your mind while you're busy building up walls around yourself. For protection"

"You have a way with words, babe," Anders told him.

"Journalism major for a reason," Trey joked. "Will you tell me what happened?"

This time, instead of dreading opening that door into his past, it felt right sharing this. The man was bringing out emotions long since buried, but he made it feel safe to dredge up the past.

"A couple of weeks after becoming a detective, I was working a kidnapping. A young boy had been reported missing from his bedroom sometime during the night. The mother realized he was gone in the morning when she went to wake him. The kidnappers had a substantial head start. We searched for days, chased down every lead, talked to the entire neighborhood, all the family members, extended and nearby. The kid's friends and their parents. The parents' friends. We left no stone unturned. The boy was well regarded by the neighbors who said he was a funny, happy little guy."

"I'm not going to like this, am I?" Trey asked.

"I can stop. It's okay."

"Not cool of me to bow out when I want to help you carry what haunts you."

Anders's body filled with warmth. How could Trey ever consider himself less than a treasure? Lucky for Anders, no one had scooped him up for their own.

"During the investigation, I began to feel like I knew this child. I'd seen his pictures, family videos, stood in his room where his toys waited for his return, talked to his daycare, family, and others who knew him. With each day that passed, the more I allowed his disappearance to invade every portion of my life. Of course, a missing child deserves my best work and all my time, but this was different. I found myself driving the streets of his subdivision at night off-hours, running scenarios through my head of how the kidnappers got in and made their getaway."

Trey squeezed his arm. "That's wasn't healthy."

"No, it wasn't. I became fixated, and decided my worth as a detective and protecting others was somehow tied up in this case. If I couldn't find this innocent child, then everything I'd ever done leading up to this case was worthless."

"Did you find him?" Trey asked, his voice barely above a whisper.

"Yeah, but not in time. As it turned out, we connected the dots to a woman having an affair with the husband. In order for them to start a new life together, they schemed to take the boy's life insurance money and hit the road."

"Shit. He did that to his own son?" Trey asked. "What about the mother? Was she involved?"

"No. She'd gotten home late the night before from her waitressing job about forty-five minutes away. Her husband told her their son was already in bed, she had no reason not to believe him, and she was so tired, she didn't check the kid's room, and went to bed. She was completely unaware her husband was having an affair, and knew nothing about the plans he'd made with this other woman. The boy had been dead before he'd been taken from the house. The autopsy ruled suffocation as the cause of death."

"Shit. Some bastards are capable of anything," Trey grumbled. "I hope they're both rotting in prison."

"The husband got life without a chance for parole considering the child had died by his hand, while the mistress got twenty-five years for conspiracy to commit first-degree murder. I got a couple of months off to get my shit together."

"They put you on administrative leave?" Trey almost shot off the bed. "You work your ass off and risk your life daily. How dare they."

"Easy tiger. No one did anything. I asked for the time off. I was at my breaking point, so I went to Oslo to be with my family. They're the reason I'm still a detective." Anders could see Trey's eyes were filling with tears.

"I'm so glad you have them." There was a loaded statement.

"Me too. They're going to love you when they meet you." Anders couldn't wait to introduce him to the family.

"Meet me?" Trey asked. "Isn't it a little soon?"

"Why? I'm happy and don't intend to go anywhere."

"So am I, but don't people usually discuss that kinda stuff several months to a year after they've been dating?"

"Who says? Anders countered. "Everybody should do what they feel in their own time. I have no idea what normal is, and, frankly, I don't want to. If there's anything you learn being a cop, it's to savor the good since we see so much shit."

"True. And it would be a stretch to say you're normal." Trey laughed.

"Hey, you're my boyfriend. You have to be nice to me."

"I didn't see that stated anywhere."

"It's in the fine print."

"Damn. They always get you with the fine print."

Anders knew Trey was trying to lift his spirits, which warmed his heart, but he could see Trey's eyelids getting heavy. "Now that I've kept my promise, it's time for you to grab a bit more sleep before dinner."

"I can't wait for the day I can stay awake a whole eight hours."

"You'll get there. Until then, you get as much sleep as you need. It's the only way to heal. You have to give your body time to get over the shock to your system."

"Okay, you win," Trey said between yawns. "This time."

"Can I get that in writing?" Anders teased, echoing Trey's words from weeks ago.

"Don't gloat." His lover smiled before closing his eyes.

Trey cuddled closer to Anders, and he welcomed the show of affection. He understood why it took a Herculean effort for Trey to trust anyone, and that Anders had been given that trust wasn't lost on him.

"I promise never to give you a reason to break your trust," Anders whispered. Trey's answering snore made him smile as he laid his head beside his lover's.

This moment of peace had been hard-fought and was well deserved.

Chapter Twelve

Trey sat on the sectional couch in the hub's living room, watching the nightly news. He was alone watching the day's events fly in fifteen-second clips. He didn't usually watch the news. He didn't own a TV. Really, he preferred to get his news online. There were a ton of news outlets, and he didn't have to listen to the talking heads babble on.

Rachel needed a new TV at the shelter to replace the old floor model built like a cabinet, which had finally given up the ghost. There hadn't been enough money in the budget to buy another one, so he gave them his. It wasn't anything special, but it was newer and worked. Since then, he hadn't bothered to replace it.

He was watching a local channel while wearing one of the many new tracksuits, which wasn't his thing, but since the people at The Gates had been kind enough to clothe him, he wasn't going to complain about what they chose. Which reminded him he needed to have a talk with Saint about Trey's apartment.

The Gates' owner had told Trey not to worry about his place, that it would be there for him when all this was over. He hadn't been able to work, and he had a feeling he knew where the rent was coming from, and who was keeping Rachel and the family afloat.

He was healing, and could stay awake longer than an afternoon. He had to get a handle on his responsibilities, and today was that day.

A flashing alert crossed the television screen, and a heavy rock settled in his stomach. The ticker line at the bottom of the screen read: *Another Body Found* above a reporter standing outside of what looked to be a deli with its side alley taped off.

He turned up the volume.

"The body of another young woman was found earlier this morning behind a Dumpster outside Vince's Deli on Broadway. Witnesses confirm the deceased was missing the index finger on her right hand. Residents and business owners want to know when this will stop and why the killer hasn't been found. Be sure to watch our Special Edition tonight at eight pm, where we delve into these and other questions."

Trey closed his eyes and buried his face in the palms of his shaking hands. Vince's Deli was only a couple blocks away from The Gates. Gary knew where Trey was, and the women of this area were no longer safe while he was here. "Why was I even born?"

"You shouldn't watch the news. They sensationalize everything for ratings." Brick's deep voice came from behind him, forcing Trey to turn in his seat.

"Regardless, there's no denying he's in this area because of me." Trey dared him to argue.

"You're right," Brick said bluntly before he walked over to the fridge to get a bottle of water.

Trey's brain screeched to a halt. Usually, people told him he wasn't responsible for Gary's actions. "You're the first one to see it my way."

"The truth's the truth no matter how you slap a bow on it. If you weren't here, Gary would be off killing someplace else." He opened the bottle and gulped down half the water.

"I guess." He hadn't thought of it that way.

"Better yet, if you'd never been born, as you stated moments ago, you wouldn't've been Gary Olsen's roommate, and he could've killed untold other girls for years. The investigation might've gone cold, and they would've had no leads."

"Okay," Trey said slowly.

Brick came around the couch and sat on the other end. "That reminds me of a man I used to know over twenty years ago. A good man, excellent battle brother. He knew what a life was worth. Every single day he wrote letters back home to his wife and young son. Hell, he'd show the little guy's picture to anyone and everyone who came within five feet. He was so proud."

Trey wasn't getting the connection. "I don't understand."

"Well, see, a few months later, we get sent on a covert mission where if you were caught, our government would deny anyone from the US military had been involved. Always loved that fucking clause. Anyway, he was shot on our way back to the rendezvous point, and no matter what our medic did to try to stop the bleeding, it was no use. By the time we made it to the helicopter, he was already in and out of consciousness. He knew he was at the end of the line, but instead of being angry or scared, he laid there and smiled. I was upset, and I asked him why he was smiling. What he said lives on to this day in my memory as if it were yesterday. He told me he wasn't afraid of death, but was sorry it came for him so soon. Opening his fist, he revealed the crumpled picture of his son and continued repeating that he wasn't disappearing from the earth. His son would carry on."

Trey cleared his throat then said, "I'm so sorry you lost your friend." This story hit so close to home with his father dying while on duty.

"So am I. He was a solid Navy Seal Captain. a good friend and mentor." Brick sucked in a deep breath and exhaled slowly. "Are you wondering why I've told you this story?"

"A bit, yeah. If it was because you needed to talk, that's okay. I'm a good listener if you need one." This could simply be about the guy needing to get things out.

Brick got a strange look on his face. "You really are so much like him."

"Who?"

"Captain Eric Stoneham."

For the first few seconds, his brain refused to kick in, and when it did, Trey had to hold onto the couch to keep himself upright. "You knew my dad? That story's about my dad?"

"Yeah. I had the honor of serving with him for several years. I'm sorry you didn't get to know him and have the time you two deserved together."

"Me too," Trey was barely holding back the tears. "Is that why you came here when Miguel asked?"

"In truth, it was me who contacted him once word got out about Sawyer's kidnapping and Miguel's involvement. Your name came up."

"Wait. Do you guys have some group or club for the retired military where you share what everyone's doing?" Since he was little, Trey wanted to know about his dad. His mother didn't talk about him, and Trey thought the guys in his dad's unit might be able to tell him what he wanted to know. But the Navy wouldn't give Trey that information, so he came up with an idea to create a military App as a way for family members to reach out to unit members. With no money, and no connections, it never got off the ground.

"Like a knitting circle? No. But we stay in contact in our ways."

"Why did you want to come here and see me?" If it was it to tell him about his father, Trey was entirely down with that.

Brick dug his right hand into an inside pocket of the jacket he was wearing, pulled out a handkerchief, and handed it to Trey. He could hear the jingle of metal sliding against metal when he adjusted it in his hand. Unsure what it was, he carefully lifted each corner one at a time until there, in the center of the handkerchief, he found a long chain with a single black military dog-tag attached.

The first line read Stoneham followed underneath by Eric H. "My dad's dog-tag."

"Yeah," Brick said solemnly. "Now you've gotta understand your mother was going through a lot at the time of your father's funeral. When I saw her drop the tag at Eric's graveside, I thought she had done it accidentally. I picked it up and rushed after her. I remember she had you in her arms. I tried to return it so that she could give it to you someday."

"She wouldn't take it."

"Right. She was suffering, so I kept it and swore if fate had our paths cross, I would return it to you."

"So when you heard my name, you contacted Miguel."

"Yeah, to confirm it was you. The next time you ask yourself why you'd been born, you have an answer."

Trey's eyes filled with tears he could no longer fight. "Thank you," he gasped as he ran the tips of his fingers over the top of the lettering in the dog-tag. His dad's service number, blood type, and division were marked.

"What the hell did you do," Anders's voice boomed through the room, making them both turn to find him and Marian standing in the doorway, "to make Trey cry?"

He looked at the situation from Anders's perspective and could understand where he was coming from. He and Brick were sitting alone on the couch, and Trey was blubbering like an idiot.

Anders stormed into the room and lifted Trey's hand to help him stand, and then wrapped his big arms around him. "Are you hurt or in pain?" he asked while giving Brick a look that should have burned a hole through his skull, but instead of looking worried, Brick sat back, his legs open, his arms outstretched across the back of the sofa.

"I'm not hurt. Brick didn't do anything to me."

"Then why are you crying?" Anders asked while still giving Brick a look that promised retribution.

"Brick gave me the best gift I've ever received," Trey explained while holding out his hand to show Anders his prize. "My dad's dog-tag."

Anders's expression changed in an instant as he looked over at Brick. "Sorry, man."

"No worries. If I had someone like him, I'd be protective too."

Trey wasn't sure what to say, so he decided to let it go. This day had gone from receiving horrible news about Gary to having a piece of the puzzle of his dad's life returned to him.

Marian came over to look at the tag and said, "Mighty fine remembrance of your father. One question, why is the metal black? I thought they all were silver."

"Special Forces, ma'am. We belonged to the same Navy Seal's unit," Brick said, still leaning back on the couch.

Marian nodded her head in understanding. "Sometimes it takes specialists even from within our military forces."

"You can let me go now," Trey suggested to Anders. "I'm fine."

"What if I don't want to?" Anders challenged with a smile.

God, Trey was falling deeper every day. Considering how they started out, that they had fallen for each other was a mystery Trey didn't want to solve.

"Why don't you take Trey back to his room, and I'll bring dinner over from the kitchen."

"I've never eaten so well," Trey said. "Thank you for everything you've done for me."

"Sweet boy, I only give people what they deserve." Marian smiled.

Before he walked out of the hub, Trey turned to Brick and said, "We're not done talking about my dad."

"Anytime, man. He's one of my fondest memories."

Chapter Thirteen

Gary watched as the woman grabbed a grocery cart before heading for the store. He drove his new van up to park directly beside her vehicle, shut off the ignition, crawled into the back, and waited.

He never did manage to steal himself a fancy car with a sunroof. He realized he wouldn't have the space and privacy to do what he needed in a car with a cutout on top. Commercial vans were the way to go. He could park them anywhere, and absolutely no one gave the van a second look.

Keeping watch through the tinted back windows allowed him to peruse his prey as they walked by. He was here for one woman specifically and didn't have time to dally with the locals. Even though a few of them had tested his resolve, he remained strong. This one was special, and worth the wait. This one could change everything.

Over thirty minutes later, she emerged from the grocery store with a cart teeming with bags. Gary got into position while keeping his eyes sharp on the surroundings to ensure no one would disturb them.

He opened both back doors and set a large, empty box on the ground before she was close enough to notice and waited with a towel soaked in chloroform clutched in his left hand. The last thing he wanted was a prolonged fight trying to get her into the back of his van, garnering attention he didn't need.

With his body concealed behind the open doors, she'd only be able to see his calves and feet from her side of the vehicle. He cocked the box to the side as she neared and pretended to struggle to get the box inside his vehicle. He even used the cane he'd found in the back of one of the vehicles he'd stolen while making a break from the overturned prison bus.

When she reached the rear of her vehicle, Gary added in a few pained groans, and with one final look around the parking lot, dropped the cane in a show to make sure she couldn't have missed it.

"Oh God, what am I going to do without my cane? I can't hold this box and reach it at the same time." He deepened his voice to sound older, and for effect, he added a few well-placed sniffles.

He knew he had her when she threw her purse into her vehicle and shut the door without unloading her groceries first. Don't worry, lady, I'm not here to rob you. Funny how someone could be so careful with their belongings but not their lives.

She came around the back of his van and bent down to pick up his cane without looking at him first. She was making this too easy. Gary shoved the box aside, and when the woman stood up, he grabbed her by her neck and covered her face in the soaked cloth.

Her struggling slowed as he dragged her into the back of the van and shut the doors. Before she drifted off to dreamland, Gary wanted to make sure she knew who had her.

"Nice to see you again, mom."

Chapter Fourteen

Anders looked at Ross, doubting he'd correctly heard the words that had come out of his mouth. "What do you mean, missing?" Alarm bells were sounding in his head, and his body went on alert.

"I mean, Rachel went to pick up groceries and never came back," Ross stated. "She'd left the house at nine this morning, and they haven't heard from her since."

"Why the hell was she going out all alone in the first place? I told her to stay in and get someone from her security detail to go. Trey's going to be devastated. Thank god he's still asleep." Anders's mind was racing in hundreds of directions. "Have you tried tracing her cellphone?"

"Yep. It led the guys to her van, which was left in the grocery store parking lot, where they found her purse locked in the back. No sign of her. We're getting the security tapes from the grocery store to see if they caught anything." Ross said.

"Gary must have been watching Rachel from the start to be there at the right moment to take advantage of the situation. The same as he'd done with Trey in the hospital." Officer Clay Everett stated. "She would've noticed the same vehicle following her around."

"Agreed," Brick said from his post in the corner. "Has anyone heard from Miguel?"

"Not since yesterday," Finn said from the couch, where members of the crew sat waiting for news.

"Wait, you wouldn't notice a work van. You know electricians' or plumbers' vans. They're all over the place in LA," Carlos said. "I've painted plenty of urban landscapes on them. They're like light posts. You know they're there, but you never really notice them."

"I'll check with burglary to see if there's been any recent thefts of commercial vans," Ross said.

"Do you honestly think he would kill his own mother?" Bradley asked from where he stood with his fiancé, Captain Meyers of the LAPD. "I mean, it's his mom." Brad's mother had taken off the moment he was born, leaving him to be raised by his grandparents. He couldn't fathom how someone else could destroy the one thing he'd craved growing up.

"Unfortunately, yes. If given a chance, he'd kill her." Anders said. "But that's not what he's going to do."

"How can you be so sure?" Clay asked as he handed Carlos a bottle of water. "He's insane and hard to predict."

"Because he wants Trey. That's his end game. It's what all this has been leading up to. Revenge." If Anders was certain of anything, it was that. "That fuckin' psycho sat stewing in prison fixated on Trey, who ended his killing spree and took his freedom away."

"What do we do now?" Saint asked as his boyfriend Max wrapped his arms around him. "How can we help?"

"There's nothing we can do," Anders growled in frustration. "We have to wait for his phone call."

"To trade Rachel for Trey?" Joey asked while his boyfriend, Officer Sam Webb, wrapped a blanket around him. Joey suffered from Sickle Cell Anemia and obviously wasn't having a good day. Anders had heard that he was scheduled to undergo a stem cell transplant later this month in an effort to slow or even stop the disease.

"That's what Gary will want," Anders agreed.

"Then that's what we'll give him," Trey's voice rose above everyone's and silenced the group.

Slowly, he walked into the living room and came to stand in front of Anders, who said, "No, we won't."

"It's not your call, detective," Trey stressed while wrapping his arms around Anders's waist. "We can't abandon her."

"I wasn't going to abandon Rachel, only come up with a different solution, which doesn't sacrifice the man I love." *Shit.* Leave it to him to screw up the time and place of sharing such a personal piece of information. Romance was a mystery to him.

"Love?" Trey asked, his head tilted back so he could look up at Anders.

Anders had never seen a room clear so quickly that wasn't a raid of some kind. Trey reached for his hand and began leading him back down the hall toward their bedroom.

Trey was silent, too silent. Was that good or bad? Definitely bad. Why the hell did he have to go and open his mouth?

Once they were inside and their bedroom door was shut, Trey didn't waste any time sinking into Anders's arms and demanding a kiss. He didn't understand what was going on, but there was no way he'd turn down a kiss from Trey.

When they finally surfaced for air, Trey declared, "I love you too."

"You do?" Anders asked as he held him at arms-length so he could see Trey's face. "You're not simply saying that because I blurted it out like a fool in front of the entire crew?"

"Nope, it's on the up and up. I love you. At first, I thought it was me rushing into things, so I kept it to myself, but now that I know you feel the same way, it's made saying so much easier." Trey was bouncing with excitement, making Anders the happiest man on the planet at that moment.

"We've only known each other for three months. It feels fast, but right at the same time. I can't be happier we're on the same page, and when we can, we're going to have one hell of a celebration." Anders smiled. "I don't care how pissed off you get, and how much you yell at me. You're not sacrificing yourself."

Trey released him and climbed into bed, and Anders followed. "If it were you, you'd be sacrificing yourself in a heartbeat to save someone's life. How is this any different?"

"Because you don't deserve to be put into this situation. You didn't sign up for that, and you damn well don't deserve to suffer another moment's pain. You've been served a raw deal from the start, and deserve to have good things happen from this point forward." Anders toed off his shoes and crawled under the covers with Trey, and then pulled him into the safety of his arms, wishing he could keep Trey there.

"I would want that too, with you by my side, but there'll be no peace for us while Gary is out there, and I wouldn't be able to live with myself if I didn't do everything in my power to save Rachel."

Anders understood and respected it. Trey's selflessness was one of the qualities that attracted Anders to him in the first place. He was fighting a war inside of himself, and no matter which side won, Anders lost, and Trey paid. Totally unacceptable.

"If you're going in, then you're going to be prepared so you can hold your own until I can get to you." Anders would make sure of it.

"Agreed," Trey said. "Now that that's settled, can we get back to we love each other before we have to take on this madman?"

**

Anders loved him. Those three words repeated in his mind on a loop. How could he be so happy while Rachel was missing? Someone he cared about was in danger, and here he was, cuddling with his lover.

"Am I a bad person?" Trey asked, unsure of how to deal with the conflicting emotions running through him.

Anders's eyes opened wide. "What? Where did that come from?"

"Rachel has been kidnapped and is in danger, and I'm lying here buzzing with happiness because you love me. Believe me, I'm still worried for Rachel and will do whatever it takes to get her back. How can I be so happy and sad at the same time?"

"You aren't even close to being a bad person, so get that out of your head. I should've picked a better time to tell you instead of blurting it out in the middle of a room full of people," Anders said before lowering his head and kissing Trey. There was a wealth of emotions behind that one kiss, and it left Trey desiring more.

He ran his hands across Anders's broad chest, desperately searching for a way under the fabric. Anders's deep growl served to spur him on searching lower until he found the hem of his shirt and slid his hands underneath. Warm skin greeted him as he ran his fingers through Anders's thick chest hair.

Their kiss deepened, and their tongues dueled as each mapped the other's mouth. Anders tasted of coffee and something sweet like candy, and he dove in for more. When they broke apart, both were panting for air. Trey took a good hard look at the man before him. The handsome devil wore that sexy grin of his effortlessly, but it was his heart and passion that drew Trey the most.

"I love you." Anders's smile was immediate. That Trey could bring him that much happiness was one hell of a confidence booster. "I want to make love with you."

"So do I. Can you, though?"

Leave it to the big guy to be worried about Trey's healing body before his own needs. "While I don't think I'm ready for calisthenics, I'm certainly up for a gentler version."

"Anything you want, as long as it doesn't cause you pain," Anders said before taking possession of his lips once again.

Trey's body was on overload. Everything from Anders's taste and scent to his touch held him entranced. He was surprised when his lover pulled away until he watched Anders slide off the side of the bed, and start to remove his clothes. It was naked time, and Trey was all for it. Trey was certain he heard a few seams tearing as Anders rushed to remove his t-shirt.

Rising at a much slower pace, Trey stood and was in the process of lifting his shirt over his head when Anders's large hands took over.

"I've gotcha," Anders said as he helped him remove his shirt without overstretching and hurting his abdomen. He'd never had someone care for him so completely.

When the fabric rose over his eyes, Trey was treated to a close-up of all that toned flesh and blond chest hair. Gods, he smelled good. The minute his arms were free, he leaned forward and sucked one of Anders's nipples into his mouth, and began flicking the hard nub with his tongue.

Anders moaned his appreciation as Trey moved over to do the same with his other nipple. The firm hand on the back of his head spurred him on, and his moans joined the chorus.

With a tug on the drawstring of his track pants, Trey felt the fabric slide down his legs. Next came his boxer briefs, and with both of Anders arms wrapped around him, he was lifted from his pile of clothing and set back on the bed.

He sat looking up at Anders as he finished undressing. His beautiful cock bobbed up and down as it was freed from its confines, causing Trey's to throb harder with need.

"You're killing me," Trey growled. "Get your sexy ass over here."

Anders's deep chuckle made Trey's heart sing, but when he went to his knees in front of Trey, he nearly swallowed his tongue. With a devilish smile, Anders spread Trey's legs and sucked his cock down his throat in one slick movement.

Trey fell back onto the bed, grabbed a pillow, and stuffed it under his head, then watched with his arms open wide as Anders's talented tongue licked the underside of his cock. The sight of the big man on his knees before him was better than any aphrodisiac, and soon his head was spinning in a fog of desire.

Far too soon, he could feel his balls tightening and that telltale tingle beginning at the base of his spine. "Babe, pull off. I'm close to coming."

It was meant as a warning to slow down, but Anders behaved like he'd been given the green light to rock Trey's world. Anders doubled his efforts as he took Trey's cock down his throat and hummed, sending him off like a rocket.

Before he had a chance to recover, Anders lifted him to the center of the bed and reached over to their bedside table. He took out a new bottle of lube and a condom from the supplies they'd purchased once they began dating.

"Are you okay?" Anders asked as he hovered over Trey. "Does anything hurt?"

"No, but I think we need to work on my stamina," Trey joked. "You were supposed to slow down when I warned you."

Anders's grin wasn't filled with contrition. "Don't worry. You'll be coming again before I'm done."

"You sound sure of yourself," Trey teased.

"Challenge accepted."

"What? Wait." Whatever Trey was about to say was swallowed up by Anders's mouth as he kissed him.

His world became centered on touches, tastes, and sounds of pleasure until the rest of the world faded to the background long enough for Trey to experience the feeling of a true moment of making love to the man he wanted to build his life with.

Anders stretched him one finger at a time while continually brushing against Trey's prostate until now he was begging to be filled. His cock grew hard under Anders generous ministrations

Trey watched with rapt attention as Anders rolled the condom over his thick cock. "How do you want me?"

"Any way I can get you," Anders responded while wiggling his brows. Who knew when they'd met that the cold Scandinavian detective was hiding his comedic and playful side under all that gruff? "Due to your injuries, I think it's best if you were on your side and I was behind you."

"Sounds perfect," Trey agreed as he leaned up for another kiss before rolling onto his side.

Anders lay behind him and began exploring Trey's shoulders and neck with his lips and tongue. Trey's body hummed with excitement as his lover's hand ghosted over his thigh and continued to his butt cheeks. A single finger delved in and brushed over his hole.

"Quit teasing me," Trey growled, his need taking hold.

The bed shook with Anders's laugh. "Yes, sir."

Trey felt the covered end of Anders's cock sliding against his skin and pushing up against his hole. He rested the side of his face onto Ander's left arm, which was under his head, and let the twinge of pain pass before Anders slid deeper.

"Yesss," Trey hissed while fisting the bedsheets.

"Remember no sudden movements or twisting. We don't want to set back your healing because we couldn't control ourselves."

"But you feel so good inside me it's hard not to move," Trey said as he fought his need to push back into his thrusts.

"I've got you, babe," Anders said before bringing his left arm up around Trey's collarbone and down over his chest to hold him still, while his right did the same with his hips.

It was like being wrapped in a bear hug while having mind-blowing sex. Trey's moans matched the thrusts into his stretched hole until it sounded like one continuous moan.

Anders's hot breath fanned the back of his neck as his lover groaned his passion. The moment felt primal, and when he bit down on Trey's shoulder, that was all it took for him to explode with a litany of colorful language.

"Damn, babe, what you do to me," Anders growled out seconds before he sunk deep into Trey and held still as he came.

Trey was happily exhausted and didn't fight the sleep when it came for him. Sometime later, he woke to find himself washed and tucked into the safety of Anders's arms as they lay in bed. His lover's loud snores could wake the dead, but Trey didn't have the heart to roll him over.

As he watched Anders sleep, Trey tried to picture going back to a life without him if he were to return to New York. Would he follow him? Would Anders want to be followed? He'd said he was ready to make a change but hadn't gone into specifics. So, it could mean anything.

Trey had to laugh at himself. *How about I get through the next couple of days alive before planning our future.* He closed his eyes and cleared his mind as much as he could. Eventually, sleep took hold, quieting his worries and buffering his dreams.

Chapter Fifteen

They didn't have to wait long for Gary's call. It came in through The Gates Restaurant phone line confirming what Trey had suspected: the psycho knew where he'd been hiding. Gary had asked for him directly.

Now here he sat staring at the telephone as if it were going to grow fangs and attack him the moment he reached for it.

"Gary is waiting," Anders said. "We have the line tapped."

Trey nodded and sucked in a deep breath before picking up the receiver, pushing the flashing red hold button, and saying, "Hello Gary."

"Trey, my old friend. It's been a long time," he said as if they were pals who hadn't seen each other in a while.

"Not long enough for me, you bastard."

"Oh, touchy, are we? Sorry to upset you, but you're not the one who they locked away, you sniveling, backstabbing dead man."

"What you were doing was wrong. You deserved to pay for what you did to those women. You had to be stopped." He had no idea why he was even bothering with an explanation.

"It was my mission, and you fucked it up. So now I'm going to fuck you up."

"Mission? What kind of fucked up mission involves killing women?" He was unable to keep his cool when faced with pure evil.

"To remove those who upset the natural order from existence. Women are the true evil in this world, and you have to cull their numbers to keep them in line. Back in college, my efforts were working. Women didn't stay out late at night, tempting weak men to their downfall. Women were in their place, inside and afraid."

Trey had to blink a few times and take a moment to let that sink in. "You believe you are called on by a higher power to protect men from the evils of women?"

"Finally, you get it. I was doing this for men like you who have resorted to dating other men because women have forgotten their place."

"Me?" Holy shit, his crazy encompassed a few phobias. What a fucking psycho nutjob. "Don't drag me into your deluded cesspool of reasons. I'm with men because it's who I'm attracted to. I was born gay and didn't suffer any humiliation at the hands of a woman to cause it."

"You don't see it. That's the problem," Olsen hissed. "Think about your relationship with your mom. How she ruined your life with her selfishness."

"My mom was suffering," Trey countered, and for the first time, he saw those events in a new light. "She lost the man she loved, was left alone to care for a small child without help and support, all the while trying to hold it all together." Shit, he was seeing things clearly now. "She fought to make it to my eighteenth birthday when she believed I'd be able to take care of myself, and the fact she held out for over sixteen years should be commended, not misconstrued into selfishness."

Trey looked up at Anders, who was watching him closely. "I get it now." His smile warmed Trey and uplifted his spirit. He was done taking his shit.

"So Gary, I suppose you want to trade your mom for me?" There was no way in hell he was going to give this evil man control over his life again. "When and where?"

There were a few seconds of silence before Gary answered, "Yes." Trey had caught him off guard, good. "Midnight tonight, behind the Hall of Records. I don't need to tell you to come alone, or Mom might find a bullet in her head."

"If there's one scratch on her, I will tear you apart," Trey threatened.

"Don't make promises you can't keep." Then the line went dead.

Anders reached around and held Trey in his arms, but for the first time, he wasn't shaking. Sure, he was afraid of Gary. He was a serial killer. But fear wasn't taking over and making it impossible for him to have a clear thought.

Anders's cell began ringing, and he dug into his pocket without removing his arm from around Trey as if he needed that connection, which Trey, sure the hell did.

"Hello."

Trey could hear the unmistakable chatter of someone talking, but couldn't make out the words. With any luck, they could pinpoint Gary's location and were calling to say they had him in custody.

"Got it, thanks." Anders ended the conversation and returned his phone to his pocket.

"Did they find him?"

Anders pulled him closer. "No. His signal was jumping between cell towers, and they couldn't get a solid lock on him."

Trey sucked in a deep breath. "Then I suppose I need to get ready."

Anders pulled Trey up from his chair and held him tight. "Not without some serious protection. There's no way I'm letting you go in there without some kick-ass self-defense measures. Let's go."

Anders took his hand, and led him from the office and back to the hub where Brick and Ross waited for them. On the table were rows of various everyday objects like a watch, ring, and glasses, as well as knives and a few things he couldn't identify.

This was where the rubber hit the road. Time for him to step up and put that crazy bastard back where he belonged for a second time. Though he had to admit the last time around he hadn't seen the truth coming. Now he knew what Gary was capable of and why he believed it was his calling. This was Trey's chance to face the creature who'd become the boogie man in his nightmares.

He'd make sure it was the last time.

***

Anders watched as Brick attached a sheathed knife to Trey's lower left leg. It was smaller than he'd expected, but it had to stay concealed under his jeans, so it made sense.

"This is a stun gun," Brick explained while holding onto a generic-looking watch. "You unscrew the top and fire it using this button." He pointed at the watch's dial and handed it over to Trey, who put it on his wrist, but then held his arm out away from his body.

"Something wrong with the watch?" Anders asked.

"I don't want to set it off accidentally," he explained, making Anders want to wrap him in bubble wrap.

"It won't go off, Trey. You have to unscrew the face of the watch to activate it," Brick explained.

"We won't be far away," Anders assured a subdued Trey. "Once the handoff is made, use whatever you have to do to put some distance between the two of you. That will give the snipers a clear shot."

None of the local LEOs were running this show. The FBI and their LAPD joint task force was handling the case and had been in to visit with Trey and go over the plan. Anders hoped they had their shit together.

"Trust me. I will. The further away from Gary, the better. I swear it." Like they were kids making a promise, Trey held out his pinky for a pinky swear. Of course, Anders grabbed it with his pinky and shook.

"This hides a metal wire," Brick said while holding out a gold ring with a school emblem on it. He slid his thumbnail under the stones and pulled out a thin wire from inside the rings hollow center. "If it comes down to up-close fighting, try to get this around his neck."

Trey took in a deep breath and slid the ring on his finger. "Got it."

"Can I have your right shoe?" Brick asked.

"Okay," Trey said as he tried to bend to undo his shoelaces.

"I got it, babe. You don't need to bend over."

"Thank you," Trey said as he held on to Anders's shoulders while he knelt in front of him to remove his shoe.

He handed the shoe to Brick, and watched as he placed a small thin device under the sole. "This will show us exactly where you are at all times."

"I like the sound of that," Trey said.

"So do I," Anders stated.

"Last, but not least, these," Brick said while holding out a pair of dark-framed glasses.

"I don't wear glasses," Trey said as he took hold of them and turned them in different angles to get a better look. "What do these do?"

"Gary won't know if you had to get corrective lenses since he last saw you. These are clear lenses without a prescription, but they will allow us to see what you see." Brick pointed to one of the small hinges. "Through here."

"This is getting more like a James Bond movie by the moment," Trey tried to smile, but couldn't manage it. Anders knew he was putting on a brave face for everyone else's benefit as he always did.

"You have no idea the range of technology available to us in special forces," Brick chuckled while he was returning a few items to a green canvas bag.

"'Cause you guys go in when the odds are against you," Trey said.

"They come in handy in those situations. Your dad was the king of gadgets. He liked to tear them apart and rebuild them. In the field, he could repair almost anything on a moment's notice."

Anders saw Trey's whole face brighten at the mention of his father. "He was handy?"

"Hell, yeah. He got us out of a few close scrapes a time or two. The man was smart. He could visualize things and reproduce them. His memory was unshakeable. If Eric confirmed someone said something or recalled what happened in the past, you knew it was true. It was uncanny." Brick became more animated when he was telling stories.

Trey put on the glasses and turned to look at Anders. "What do you think? Am I ready?"

Anders ran his hands down Trey's shoulders and said, "No, you're missing something."

Trey's brows furrowed as he looked himself up and down, trying to figure out what he was missing. "What?"

Anders dug his hand into his jean pocket and pulled out Trey's father's dog-tag, which had been placed in a small jewelry box on their dresser for safekeeping, and placed it around Trey's neck. "Now, you're ready. Your dad would be so proud of you and your courage."

"Courage? I'm shaking in my shoes." Trey looked at him like he'd grown a third eyeball.

"Listen to me. Courage doesn't mean you are without fear. Courage is carrying on despite it." Anders brushed the palm of his hand against Trey's cheek. "You've lived your entire life with courage."

Trey took a step toward him, and Anders engulfed him in his arms. He fought the urge to wrap up this amazing man and lock him in his room. They'd taken every precaution. Put undercover cops on the streets, snipers on the rooves, LAPD were waiting blocks away in delivery vans acting as the FBI's back-up. They even had officers placed around the area as homeless people pushing old grocery carts or lying in local buildings' alcoves on cardboard. Trey was a walking arsenal with weapons hidden all over his body.

Yet, Anders was ready to throw up.

When they released one another, he realized Brick had gone, giving them their privacy. "You know how much I love you?"

Trey's smile was instantaneous. "Yeah, I know, and I love you too."

"When this is all over, how about we shack up together and get our own place," Anders suggested. He'd been thinking about it for weeks. There was no way in hell he was returning to New York without Trey, and considering the bad memories he had of New York, LA was the better option.

"You're going to move to LA?" Trey asked. "Like right away."

"Yeah as soon as I can. I have to go back to New York to fill out the paperwork to resign from the NYPD. Then I have to organize moving my stuff out here, and paying out the end of my lease." Trey looked like he was getting ready to interrupt, and Anders hurried to say, "It's not too bad, I have two months left. While I'm in New York, I'll start applying to various law enforcement agencies in LA and surrounding counties. I want to be where you are. I told you I was open to change, and I meant it. So, back to my question. Condo, apartment, or townhouse?"

Trey laughed as Anders had hoped. "Anywhere you are, works for me."

"Here to serve," Anders said and gave him a salute for good measure.

"It's expensive to live in LA. Maybe we should live in an apartment to start. I don't have a reliable source of income." Trey looked embarrassed by his meager wages. There was no way Anders would ever allow him to feel "less than" anymore.

"I have money saved up that'll get us something reasonable, and safe." He squeezed Trey's hands. "Remember, I have to get a job, and that won't happen overnight."

"Don't worry. I'll contribute my share, I promise."

"We will work together and figure everything out. How does that sound?"

"Sounds like a deal?"

"Deal."

Chapter Sixteen

According to the bank's flashing clock, the night was cold by California standards. He'd lived through winters in New York, so this was not what he'd personally consider freezing as native Californians described it. Wusses.

The streets were reasonably quiet as he walked towards the corner of Temple and Hill Streets. He had to admit he didn't know much about the Hall of Records or why Gary would want to meet him there.

Every time he crossed someone's path, he wondered if that person were a police officer or someone who was going to mug him. It was midnight in DTLA, and not everyone on the streets had good intentions. However, no one made eye contact with him except for the beggar on the corner. If there were officers out here, no one was breaking character.

He passed the Courthouse on his way down Hill Street. The occasional window in the surrounding tall buildings was lit from within, and company signs flashed and shone in a variety of colors. Still, other than those and the street lights, it felt overly dark for some reason. Trey had to wonder if it was his mind playing tricks on him, considering what he was about to do and who was waiting for him.

If he looked at his life in its entirety, Trey couldn't've predicted the moment he found true happiness would be the moment he had to face the horrors of his past. He lifted his hand to take hold of his dad's dog tag, centering himself as he neared Grand Park, which ran along both sides of Hill Street.

Trey continued scanning the area as he neared Temple Street. Still, nothing stood out. His heart was trying to race its way out of his chest, and his stomach was rolling. Shortly before reaching

Temple Street, he took a short staircase to the right up to a courtyard behind the Los Angeles County Hall of Records. He slowed and began looking around for any sign of Gary and Rachel. Nighttime made the most innocent of objects look edgy and dangerous, and the breeze became whispers.

Movement caught his attention, and he slowly made his way to a small separate standalone structure, which didn't look to have a purpose. The last thing he wanted to do was to come up on some gang members hanging in the park conducting business. That would not end well for him.

As he got closer to the building, Trey realized Rachel was standing slightly below street level in front of an old elevator. The sign above reading, 222 N. Hill Street. Her face was pale, and she had a bruise on her cheek, but other than that, he couldn't see any other damage.

"Rachel?" Trey whispered as he descended the stairs. "Are you okay?"

"She is for now," Gary's harsh raspy voice sliced through the quiet night. "As long as you don't try anything stupid and get her shot. Now get over here and take her place before I change my mind," he ordered, revealing his position and his gun from the dark corner where the streetlights didn't reach.

Trey raised his hands and continued forward until he was standing in front of Rachel.

"I'm sorry, Trey," she said as her lips trembled and her eyes filled with tears. "I never meant for this to happen."

"I know, it's going to be okay," Trey assured even though he was far from certain.

"I'll be the judge of that," Gary growled as he came up behind him and wrapped his hand around Trey's throat. His fingers dug into his Adam's apple while pressing the muzzle of his handgun to Trey's temple.

"You're free to go, mom. It's been nice catching up. We'll have to do it again sometime," Gary quipped as he walked Trey backward toward the elevator. Where the hell were they going? When the asshole pushed the elevator button, Trey got truly nervous. Why would Gary trap himself in this building?

When the bell sounded, and the doors slid open, Rachel turned around, tears running down her face, and watched as Gary dragged him inside. At least she was safe now. The police would find her in no time, thanks to his glasses showing them exactly where to find her.

He was positive there'd be a round bruise where Gary had the gun jammed on the side of his face. "Where are we going?" Trey asked as the killer pushed the number 2 button, and they began going down.

"Somewhere a little more private."

When the doors opened, Trey found himself walking out into some sort of tunnel system. What the hell was this doing here?

"What is this?"

"The tunnels under the city," he answered while shoving Trey forward. "Keep moving."

They turned right and followed an escalator up one level as the labyrinth revealed itself. *Shit, how is Anders supposed to find me in there?* Now that he thought about it, Trey remembered hearing old stories of how they used to move alcohol through here during prohibition in the 1920s to the speakeasies.

Rows of pipes ran across the ceiling into the distance. They passed row after row of locked, fenced-off corridors. Their footsteps echoed as steam hissed, and vents spread hot air throughout. There was more rubble lying around the further they went until they came to one fence that had its lock cut.

Gary pushed him through the open fence as he was trying to get a good look around so that his rescue party could find him. "Move it."

Trey had to ask him the question that had been burning in his brain while he had the chance. "Why are you risking your freedom by coming after me? You had to know the police would be watching me."

"You are the proof of my failure. I can't carry on with my mission while you're alive," Gary answered as if that were completely logical while he shoved Trey forward over a stack of old boxes. His bones rattled when his body hit the concrete floor causing him to cry out in pain. For a moment, he lost his breath, and was gasping for air as Gary's maniacal laughter echoed around them.

When he managed to get on his feet, the dis,tinctly iron taste of blood filled his mouth. His lip was cut, and his jaw ached, but considering he fell face first, he was lucky to come away without a broken nose. Unfortunately, his glasses didn't fare so well as they sat crushed on the concrete. As for his stomach, a new pulsing pain began radiating from his right side. Not good.

Stay on track. "How am I proof of your failure?" He had to keep Gary talking until either he was saved or figured out a way to break free.

"I allowed you into my world against my better judgment, and you betrayed me. If I allowed you to live, what does that say about me?"

"That you're regaining sanity?" Trey had no idea why he was goading the asshole, but he was reaching his breaking point fast.

"It says I have no control, no power over what you did to me. You took my manhood away. You castrated me as good as any woman could. With you dead, I take back my control, my strength, and power. With you dead, I can begin anew with my mission." There was a gleam in his eyes when he spoke about his *mission,* and it made Trey's already tormented stomach turn.

Yeah, there was going to be no reasoning with Gary. Force it was, then. "How do you think you're going to make it out of here? There are cops everywhere looking for you."

"There are entrances and exits if you know where to look and miles of tunnel for your friends to search. Don't worry about me."

"I wasn't. I was trying to get you to see reason. If you let me go—"

"You're not going anywhere. Turn left up here. We aren't far now."

Far from what? Where he'd be killed? I don't think so.

The feel of the cold metal being pressed against his spine had him rethinking the whole fighting back plan, but he quickly pulled himself together. He had a life to build with Anders, and a future that he was looking forward to. He wouldn't allow this psycho to keep on killing, and he wouldn't allow him to take away what Trey had worked for.

Roughly, twenty paces after they turned left, Trey came to a familiar sight he'd never wanted to see again. The altar had the same type of burned candles as Gary's original one had, and it also included the severed fingers of his victims. All but the one he'd delivered to Trey in the hospital.

Okay, he wasn't sticking around to find out what happened next. He didn't hear the cavalry coming, so it was all on him. Trey raised his wrist to his chest and pointed his watch outward, removed the cover, and placed his finger on the dial. Knowing you're about to die was one hell of a motivator to try out Brick's gizmos.

"Take a good look around. This will be the last place you will ever see," Gary's voice was almost gleeful, sending chills down Trey's back. "I've been looking forward to the day I could choke the life out of you."

This was it. Time to grab his courage by the balls. After one last tap on his dad's tags for courage and a picture of Anders in the forefront of his mind, Trey turned around.

***

Anders watched as the elevator doors closed tight. His heart was racing, and he needed answers. "Where is he taking Trey?"

"Looks like he's come up from the tunnels," Ross answered as the channels lit up.

"Tunnels in LA?"

"Leftovers from prohibition and gangsters," one of the FBI Agents stationed in front of a screen provided.

He watched on the monitor as officers converged on the scene and took Rachel to a nearby ambulance to be checked over

"Tell me we have officers in the tunnels," Anders demanded, and when the guys remained silent, he burst out of the back of the delivery truck and ran down the block to the Hall of Records.

Logically, he knew Trey had a tracker on him, but it wasn't enough if Gary decided to shoot him before help could arrive. When he reached the elevator, he flashed his badge at the officers securing the location and pushed the button.

"Detective Nilsen, we haven't secured the tunnel yet. You could be walking into a trap," an officer said as the door chimed and opened.

He stepped into the elevator, removed his gun from its holster, and was about to press the same button he'd seen Gary press with the help of Trey's glasses when he heard Ross hollering. Anders looked up to find the detective running for the elevator.

"You're not going down there alone," Ross said as he joined Anders in the elevator. "Do you even know where you're going?"

"Down," Anders growled while pushing the number two button. He should never have let Trey face that maniac alone.

Now it was a race to reach his love in time, and there was no way he was going to let Trey down.

Chapter Seventeen

Trey stared at Gary for a moment before pushing the dial and releasing the electrodes that quickly attached themselves to the evil man's chest and arm. Gary's eyes opened in shock, but it was too late to avoid what was coming.

His body convulsed as the first few hits of electricity coursed through his body. The gun Gary had been holding fell to the ground seconds before he did. Trey was quick to remove the watch, jumped over the asshole, and ran out of the corridor.

Not once did he look back, figuring gaining distance between them was the best plan, so he ran blindly forward until the passageways began to all look alike. He was lost in an underground tunnel system with an armed madman hunting him down. *Shit. Shit. Shit.*

Finally, he slowed to try to get his bearings and to listen for footsteps coming up behind him. Thankfully, he heard nothing. The tunnel he was in looked older than some of the others he'd walked through. The concrete was breaking apart, and the walls were covered in faded paint, and there were words etched into the walls. A few busted wooden tables lay strewn across the floor along with dirt and crumpled old newspapers.

It appeared no one had been down here in a long time.

Trey continued down the tunnel, but gave up running as his body struggled to stay upright. He continued on as quietly as possible, desperate not to give himself away. He stepped carefully, trying to hear if anyone was coming. More old tables and chairs made him wonder if this was one of the Prohibition places.

He didn't have time to stop and explore. Trey had to find a way out before Gary caught up to him. When he turned the next corner, he spotted something that looked like stairs and headed straight for them. However, he only made it halfway.

"Trey?" Anders's voice echoed around him, and he turned to find his lover only a couple of dozen feet away coming out of another tunnel. "Thank god, I found you."

Anders was a sight for sore eyes even though they'd only been apart for a few hours. Trey could feel his body relaxing as he drew near. "I'm so happy to see you. Have they arrested Gary?"

"That would be, no." Gary's voice broke through his happiness as quickly as a hot knife through butter. "Drop the gun and go stand by Trey." He ordered, coming out of the tunnel behind Anders.

Anders slowly dropped his handgun and raised his hands into the air. His face was a mixture of anger and concern as he neared Trey. "I'm sorry, babe."

"It's not your fault."

Anders placed his body in front of Trey's using himself as a human shield when he reached him. Trey wouldn't allow it and stood out from behind Ander's.

"We're a team. We'll face this together."

Ander's nodded and took hold of Trey's hand. "Together."

"Ahhh isn't that sweet," Gary cackled, and it had the same effect as nails on a chalkboard. "Willing to die together. So romantic."

"You know you're never making it out of these tunnels without being taken into custody," Anders said in a surprisingly calm voice. "Officers are combing the tunnels. There's no way out."

For the first time, Trey saw a kink in his former roommate's armor. His eyes darted from side to side as he thought over what Anders had said. "We need to move."

"To where? No place is safe for you," Anders continued.

"Shut up," Gary growled. "Or…"

"Or what, you'll shoot us. You can't do that if you want to bargain your way out of here."

Trey stood back and watched as Anders used his skills to convince Gary he needed them alive. His voice never rose or changed in modulation. There was no emotion, only facts. It was amazing watching his lover get into the killer's head.

"I don't need both of you," he said as he raised his gun and pointed it at Anders's head.

"If you kill an officer of the law, there's no way you're getting out of here alive." Trey scrambled to think of something to stop him from pulling the trigger. "It would be easier to exchange him for free passage out of here."

Trey knew he was talking out of his ass, but if he played his cards right, he might be able to convince Gary not to shoot. The gun shook slightly as he thought over his options.

"Then I don't need you," he growled. "Goodbye, Trey." Gary pointed his gun at Trey's head.

"Put down the gun." A voice boomed Trey had never been happier to hear. Miguel.

Sure enough, across the tunnel stood Miguel holding a rifle pointed at Gary's head. Trey's moment of happiness was shattered when Gary smiled. He'd made his choice.

The next thing Trey knew, he was falling, and guns were firing. It didn't take him long to realize Anders had seen Gary's smile and covered Trey with his body as protection.

When Anders didn't move, Trey suspected the worst, but as soon as Miguel gave the all-clear, his lover leapt off of him and began checking Trey for injuries.

"Are you hurt?" He was frantically moving Trey's clothes to the side to get a better look at him.

Trey gave his body a once over and had to admit his abdomen was tender, but he expected that considering he'd been pushed over a box onto the concrete.

"No, I'm not hurt. My mid-section hurts, but that was from Gary earlier. Are you hurt?"

"It's only a scrape," Anders said. "We need to have you checked out."

He batted Anders's hand and said, "Let me see this scrape."

Anders moved over to the side and helped Trey to his feet. Trey saw Gary's lifeless body crumpled onto the ground with Miguel standing guard. He could hear more people headed in their direction, but all that mattered was his lover.

"Show me this scratch."

Anders turned around, and Trey got his first look at the "scratch." A flesh wound roughly four inches long tracked the bullet's trajectory across Anders's back. His shirt was torn, and he was bleeding, but it looked to be no worse than a bad cut.

"You would've taken a bullet for me?"

"Well, yeah. I love you," he said as if it were a foregone conclusion.

"I love you, too, you crazy-ass Viking," Trey said as he gathered Anders into his arms. "How about we pick up a newspaper on the way back to The Gates and start shopping for our new apartment."

"Sounds like the perfect plan," Anders agreed as he buried his face into the side of Trey's neck.

"Deal."

"Deal."

***

Anders watched as Dr. Green gave Trey a top to bottom check over. He'd refused to have his injury looked at until Trey was seen to first. Now that that was happening, a nurse was headed his way to clean out his wound and check if he needed stitches.

When an orderly came to take Trey down to imagining, Anders stood to follow, much to the nurse's surprise.

"Detective Nilsen, please sit back down so I can finish cleaning your wound. "

Trey looked over from his wheelchair and said, "I'll be okay. It won't be long."

Grudgingly Anders sat and watched the clock like a hawk. He'd give them fifteen minutes to take the images and bring Trey back before he went looking. He couldn't curb his reactions after almost losing the man he loved. He didn't even try. It would be a long time before Anders would feel comfortable having Trey out of his sight.

Dr, Green came over to have a look at his wound and decided it didn't require stitches, so they put a few Steri Strips over the wound and called him good to go. The clock was thirty seconds away from hitting the fifteen-minute mark when they wheeled Trey back in.

"I'm surprised you didn't come looking for me," Trey teased as he climbed up onto his hospital bed. "How long did I have?"

Anders couldn't help but smile. His lover knew him well. "Fifteen minutes," he replied as he pulled a chair closer to Trey's bed. "How do you feel?"

"Tired."

"Why don't you lay your head down and get some rest. I won't leave your side."

"Thanks. I think I will. It's getting hard to keep my eyes open."

Anders reached over and began running his fingers through Trey's hair as his breathing evened out, and he began snoring. As the silky strands slipped through his fingers, he noticed there was red mixed in with the brown. Trey had once said his hair was boring brown when in truth, red was intermixed, making his hair officially auburn.

Like his hair, Trey viewed himself as one dull tone when he had layers of colors inside him. Anders wanted to be there the day his lover figured that out for himself.

Dr. Green walked into the room, and Anders quickly motioned that Trey was asleep before the doc could start talking. He nodded his head and motioned toward Trey's abdomen before making a thumbs-up sign.

Anders felt a weight lift off his shoulders. Trey hadn't been reinjured and wouldn't require any further surgeries. Now that his stress was lowered, Anders own exhaustion was kicking in like a tidal wave.

He gave in to the struggle and lowered his head to his arm lying on Trey's bed, and reached for his love's hand. He placed his other arm over top of Trey's thighs so he could register any movement before closing his eyes and letting the world fade away.

Everything he would ever need was safely in his arms.

Epilogue

The sun was shining, and there wasn't a cloud in the sky. The day had turned out better than Trey could've ever imagined. The yard wasn't huge by any means, but the children raced between the tables playing games and laughing while the adults were busy setting out the buffet, cooking on the barbeque, or sitting in lawn chairs talking.

Trey scanned the group, happy to see his two worlds melding together. Marian, Captain Meyer's mom, Bradley's grandmother, and Rachel sat back while everyone else got everything set up. Alexander and Sawyer were busy on the grill while Bobby directed where the food should be placed on the long table. The guy had mad organizational skills.

Saint and Max stood talking with the guys who watched out for the home's women and children while Bradley's three-legged dog chased a ball around the backyard. Even the neck tattoo guy had a smile on his face. Sam and Joey couldn't be here because Joey was still in the hospital after his stem cell therapy.

Miguel and Carlos were overseeing the children's small crafts table while Finn and Clay watched on, both smiling. Trey couldn't help but smile as well at the sight of the two large men sitting at a child-sized table covered in glitter, paint, and glue.

Detective Ross and his boyfriend James, along with Brick and Captain Meyers, were in the living room putting on a display of self-defense techniques for the women living at the shelter. They'd set up training mats and everything. At the same time, Detective Ross's sister Jo and her daughter were busy in the sandbox surrounded by children making sandcastles. Brick would be leaving in the morning for Texas, and Trey had to admit he would miss the guy. The stories he'd shared with Trey about his dad helped solidify the image he'd been carrying around in his head.

It all seemed too fantastical. If he'd been told this lunch would happen, Trey wouldn't've believed it. It'd been six months since his showdown with Gary Olsen, and with each passing day, his world brightened a little bit more.

He no longer lived in fear, scrounging for every last penny he could earn. In a weird turn of events, Cooper Hitchford's family had given a large donation to the shelter as a gift, and perhaps penance for what their son had done, which had nearly killed Trey. He felt for the Hitchfords. He knew all about carrying the guilt for someone else's behavior, and he understood their need to do something positive to try to balance the scales.

"Are you going to put that down?" Anders's voice brought him back to the here and now. "Or are you hoarding for yourself?"

Trey looked down and realized he'd been standing in front of the buffet, holding a large bowl in his hands. "Oh." He laughed as Anders shook his head and gave him the grin that made Trey melt. Their new apartment in Riverside wasn't fancy, but it was clean and safe. The two mandatory features neither of them would compromise on.

It had taken Anders over two months to finalize everything back in New York, and then another two months of interviews and background screenings before he was hired by the Riverside County Sheriff's office. The county was fifty miles east from DTLA and ran along the Santa Ana River. As of yet they hadn't dropped by the famous Mission Inn, but it was on the list of must-do's according to Carlos, who'd painted a few canvases there.

Trey had been fortunate enough to net an entry level position with *The Press-Enterprise*, a local news outlet. For the first time in his life, he was using his journalism degree for hard-hitting news and not filler pieces. Happy didn't scratch the surface of what he was feeling. They were living their best lives.

"Whatcha got there, Trey?" Bobby asked.

With a huge smile, he said, "Pot stickers. Anders's favorite."

His lover's eyes opened wide, but before he could deny it, Bobby said, "Great, I'll make sure you get a good share, Detective Nilsen."

"Uh… thanks for thinking of me." Anders shrugged as Trey set down the bowl where Bobby had instructed.

The moment they were alone again, Anders grabbed his hand and led him over to the side of the house. "Pot stickers, I thought you loved me."

Trey couldn't help but laugh at his lover's pout. "Put that bottom lip away, detective. Of course, I love you. I want to spend my life with you, which brings me to this."

He dug into the pocket of his jeans as he tried to calm his racing heart. His fingers touched the metal, and he pulled it free before holding it up between them. Anders's expression was a map of emotions.

"What do you think? Wanna get hitched?" Trey's voice sounded a whole lot calmer than he truly felt. He never took into account the possibility Anders might say no.

The seconds ticked by like a bell sounding in his head.

When Anders opened his mouth, it wasn't to say the word yes. "On one condition."

"Condition?"

"One," he said, then placed another gold band beside the first. "That you say yes to me."

Trey didn't know how they managed to both get rings for the same day, but he knew exactly what to say.

"Deal."

"Deal," Anders repeated.

Trey slid his ring onto his love's finger, and then Anders did the same. Before they had a chance to kiss, Marian came around the corner. She eyed their hands and nodded her head.

"Told you to keep a close eye on him, detective."

"Yes, ma'am, you did, and I intend to for the rest of my life," Anders stated with a confident smile.

"Well done, young man," she said before turning around to leave. "Now kiss him, already."

"Yes, ma'am." Anders smiled before taking Trey's mouth.

This was love. This was family, and he'd never take it for granted.

BONUS

TURN THE PAGE AND TAKE A SNEAK PEEK AT
THE FIRST BOOK IN MY NEW SERIES:

FIRE LAKE

We're heading back to Texas. Yee-Haw.

BRICK

The house looked much the same as he remembered from his childhood. Except for the years of rot, infestation, overgrowth, and dirt. They were new unwelcome additions.

The large wrap-around porch looked ready to crumble if someone dared to step on the boards. Large single-pane windows, which had long ago lost their seals, and any energy efficiency they might have had, were either broken or cracked. The shutters were hanging by sheer will alone, at least the ones still attached to the faded board and battered exterior.

Brick got out of his truck and stood in the long laneway as he tried to wrap his head around the truth: he was the lake house's new owner. His Great Aunt Sophia, god rest her soul, had passed away two years ago while he was overseas during a tour of duty. She'd left him this place for some unknown reason, and today marked the day he moved in.

He heard animals scurrying underneath the steps as he carefully navigated his way onto the porch and to the large, ornately carved front door. That would have to stay once it had been restored.

He'd enjoyed the time he'd spent at The Gates and took in a lot of information regarding the restoration going on with the condo conversion. Max of Connor Construction had been a wealth of information and said he'd come down and take a look at the place if Brick needed any help. Stand-up guys over there in California, that was for sure.

The boards creaked underneath his boots as he pulled out the key and unlocked the front door. The stale air assailed him, and years of dust was layered over everything. Sheets covered most of the items in the living room and dining room, but the kitchen looked the same as when his aunt had been alive.

There was an empty mug sitting beside the old six-cup coffee machine. Newspapers from over two years ago were piled on the counter, and a single chair was pulled back from the kitchen table as if waiting for his great aunt's return. Even her bedazzled cane stood leaning against the wall.

It'd crushed Brick when he couldn't make it back for her funeral. At the time, he was deep behind enemy lines on a mission. She had been so proud when Brick became a Navy Seal, though she didn't like the danger he lived mission to mission. Brick could still remember her cheering him on when he walked up to the podium to have his gold trident pinned to his uniform.

He wandered the rooms in the basement, and the ground and second floors, trying to develop a plan. What was he going to do with all this room and the ten acres of forested waterfront land that came with it? Brick stopped in the front room with its wall of windows facing Fire Lake. The view was stunning, with its large red cedars and oaks framing the calm waters. The sound of water lapping at the shoreline was a melody Brick had fallen asleep to on numerous occasions. He remembered catching bass out of that lake for his great aunt to fry up.

She'd always made a big deal every time he returned with a catch or two. She'd prepare them a special way, which she never shared, and set out the good china even though it was usually only the two of them. Brick had loved visiting Sophia. Even as he grew older, he'd make sure to visit as often as he could.

Though he knew she would've understood why he couldn't come back while she was sick, he was a long way from forgiving himself for not being there when she needed him. It didn't matter that other family members were with her when the end came. He wasn't, and that was unforgivable.

Brick opened the back garden doors and stepped out into the waning sunlight. Sophia's prized flower beds were overgrown, while her climbing roses grew wild into the surrounding bushes. The stone birdbath was missing its pedestal, and the garden shed's roof had caved in. The yard hadn't been mowed in years and reached all the way up to his knees.

The more he looked, the more he found what needed fixing, cleaning, cutting, replacing, or exterminating. This was what happened when a building was left to sit without life in it. The same held true for people.

As he neared the water, the chorus of ducks grew louder in the quiet of the twilight descending around him. The rich loamy smell of the earth and water drew him closer, and a patch of bluebonnets stood in vivid contrast to the green surroundings.

Brick could almost hear Sophia telling the younger him to leave the bluebonnets alone after one misguided flower picking session. That was the day he learned the pretty, little plant which grew wild was toxic.

Sitting on the sizable rocks at the water's edge, Brick took a minute to get his head on straight. He couldn't keep the house. It was way too big for one person and required too much work to make it livable. He'd already spent a large portion of his life amid destruction. He didn't think he really wanted to take this on.

He ran his palm over one of the rocks' rough surfaces when he felt grooves in the surface. Leaning over, he took a closer look at the marks and almost fell off his rock when he found his great aunt's name chiseled into the stone. It wasn't professionally done, more like a backyard hammer and chisel job. Had Sophia left that here?

Upon further inspection, he found more marks on another portion of the rock and squinted to make out the letters in the last bit of light. Christopher. His legal first name. It appeared Sophia chiseled his name on the rock as well.

There was a month and date inscribed underneath his name. Brick thought he was seeing things, but he used his fingertip to trace the numbers. Sure enough, it was dated the same month Sophia had been hospitalized. That meant one of her final acts was to've added his name.

His hand shook as he brushed the engraving one last time before standing and looking back at the lake house.

"Shit. I can't believe I'm going to do this." He took a deep breath and headed back to the house. This could be the beginning of the best decision he'd ever made, or the expressway to his destruction.

Brick opened the garden doors and stood in the middle of the main floor as he took stock of everything around him.

Home, Sweet Home.

AUTHOR'S NOTE

This story ends The Gates series. I wanted to take a moment and thank all of you for joining me and the characters on their journeys. We helped a man rediscover himself, and another to find a home and acceptance. We danced at a wedding, ended a crime family's rule, and slew old demons for more than a few people.

Along the way, we watched as the crew from The Gates navigated love, loss, and new beginnings, including the restoration of a beloved building back to its former glory. A true reflection of the downtown as a whole – a snapshot in time.

The City of Angels is more than the playground for the rich and famous. Lives play out every day far away from the glitter and glam: gritty, raw, and real, lightyears from the golden Malibu hills seen on every postcard, or the landmark Hollywood sign.

We explored living on the streets struggling with homelessness, serious illnesses, mental breakdowns, heroic actions, loyalty, and the true meaning of family. I hope I've done the city justice, and all the wonderfully unique people who call it home.

Below is a picture I took while visiting DTLA with my amazing publisher and friend, Michelle. This building became my inspiration for The Gates.

ABOUT THE AUTHOR

M. Tasia is a M/M romance author who lives in Ontario, Canada. She's is a dedicated people watcher, lover of romance novels, 80's rock, and happily-ever-afters (once the MCs are put through their paces, of course), who grew up with a love of reading. She's a firm believer that everyone deserves to have love, excitement, and crazy hot romance in their lives. Love should be celebrated and shared.

Connect with M.:

mtasiabooks.com

facebook.com/mtasiabooks

twitter.com/mtasiaauthor

instagram.com/m.tasia.author/

www.BOROUGHSPUBLISHINGGROUP.com

If you enjoyed this book, please write a review. Our authors appreciate the feedback, and it helps future readers find books they love. We welcome your comments and invite you to send them to info@boroughspublishinggroup.com. Follow us on Facebook, Twitter and Instagram, and be sure to sign up for our newsletter for surprises and new releases from your favorite authors.

Are you an aspiring writer? Check out www.boroughspublishinggroup.com/submit and see if we can help you make your dreams come true.

www.ingramcontent.com/pod-product-compliance
Lightning Source LLC
Chambersburg PA
CBHW071320130626
46556CB00004B/1672